VALENTINE FOR A
DEAD LADY

Library and Archives Canada Cataloguing in Publication

Ames, Mel D., 1921-
[Short stories. Selections]
    Valentine for a dead lady / Mel D. Ames.

(Dime crime ; volume 1)
Short stories originally published in Mike Shayne mystery magazine.
Issued in print and electronic formats.
ISBN 978-1-77161-070-4 (pbk.).--ISBN 978-1-77161-071-1 (html).--
ISBN 978-1-77161-072-8 (pdf)

    I. Title.

PS8551.M47A6 2014   C813'.54   C2014-904622-7
                                             C2014-904623-5

Pubished by Mosaic Press, Oakville, Ontario, Canada, 2014.
Distributed in the United States by Bookmasters (www.bookmasters.com).
Distributed in the U.K. by Gazelle Book Services (www.gazellebookservices.co.uk).

MOSAIC PRESS, Publishers
Copyright © 2014 Mel D. Ames

Printed and Bound in Canada.
ISBN Paperback 978-1-77161-070-4
          ePub 978-1-77161-071-1
          ePDF 978-1-77161-072-8

Designed by Eric Normann

We acknowledge the financial support of the Government of Canada through the Canada Book Fund (CBF) for this project.

Nous reconnaissons l'aide financière du gouvernement du Canada par l'entremise du Fonds du livre du Canada (FLC) pour ce projet.

 Canadian Heritage Patrimoine canadien

 Canada

MOSAIC PRESS
1252 Speers Road, Units 1 & 2
Oakville, Ontario L6L 5N9
phone: (905) 825-2130

info@mosaic-press.com

www.mosaic-press.com

VOLUME 1

VALENTINE FOR A DEAD LADY

MEL D. AMES

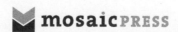
mosaicPRESS

Contents

A Matter of Observation

Originally published in *Mike Shane Mystery Magazine*, November 1980.

ROOM 804, AT THE HOTEL WESTMORE, HARBORED A GRIM pantomime of death. The nude body of a woman hung from a light fixture, by the neck, and an overturned chair lay within kicking distance of a dainty, pedicured foot. There was an eerie attitude to the body; to the limbs, mostly, as they stood out a little from the perpendicular. It was as though death had come suddenly in a throe of panic. The weight of the body on the thin leather belt from which it hung, had pulled the light fixture partly away from the ceiling, and a few pieces of plaster were strewn on the dark pile of carpet. Some of the plaster fragments, between the rungs of the overturned chair and beneath the body, were scrunched deeply into the rug fibers. The room was furnished with the usual, tiresome trappings, peculiar to all second-rate hotels: bed, dresser, night table, a mate to the fallen chair, and a television set. The rapid flip-flopping of the TV screen gave a weird, psychedelic aspect to the scene, and a tuneless rock-group, blaring from the FM band, seemed only to fuel the illusion.

Detective-Lieutenant Cathy Carruthers stood in the open doorway, surveying the room with a cold, calculating eye. No sign of emotion, no feminine impropriety, marred the composure of her finely-wrought features. She was six feet from head to heel, and blonde; and as she paced the hotel room in silent deliberation, she did things to a straight-cut, gray business suit that had never been intended. And even though the garment ended mid-thigh, it fell well short of its given purpose; to subdue, and otherwise divert attention from the superb body that moved within it. Her vital statistics had become classified information at Metro Central's Eleventh Precinct.

"Suicide?"

Detective-Sergeant Mark Swanson regarded his partner with manly deference. The questioning tone in his voice had not been unintentional, though the fact seemed self-evident. Bitter experience had taught him to accept the obvious with caution.

It had not been that way to begin with. But in recent months, he had found many compensations working with the 'Amazon,' an epithet that had been bestowed upon her (with affection) from her burly colleagues in Homicide. Mark had felt no sense of umbrage in their gender disparity, nor was he phased by the constant derision he endured at the hands of his macho cohorts. In addition to her obvious physical attributes, he had found his new partner to be a highly engaging individual and a detective of rare acumen.

"Shall I cut her down, lieutenant?"

"Do that, Mark." Her smile was butter on his daily bread. "Use the same chair."

Mark set the chair upright, beside the hanging woman. The pointed toes hung about an inch below the level of the seat. "With that kind of clearance," he said, "she'd have had to stand on tip-toe. A bit of a stretch, but certainly not impossible."

Lieutenant Carruthers winced with womanly qualm as her partner mounted the chair, sinking his feet deep into the well-up-holstered cushion—with typical masculine indifference, she thought—but then returned her attention to the dead woman, as he parted the thin leather belt that held her, and lowered her gently to the floor.

She had been pretty, once, about mid-twenties, with short dark hair and a good figure. Now, her face was a purple horror. The lieutenant knelt beside the body and drew a few strands of tightly curled hair from one clenched fist.

"Could be her own," Mark observed, over her shoulder. The lieutenant turned contemplative eyes upon him that temporarily took his mind off his work. This was one of the compensations.

"Take a sheet from the bed and cover her," she said demurely, slipping the hair samples into a small white envelope, then into her jacket pocket.

A little man with black hair and swarthy features came into the room. "My name's Forbes," he said curtly, "I'm the hotel manager." He leveled his words at Mark, who, busy with the sheet, directed him with a nod of the head to his imposing colleague.

"Thank you for coming," said the lieutenant, pleasantly, "I should like to ask you a few questions."

The little man turned his head from one to the other, unable to decide where his obeisance lay. Cathy Carruthers had long since resigned herself to this hesitancy on the part of some men in accepting her, a woman, in what they considered a man's domain. But precious few hesitated for long.

"What was the woman's name?" she asked with practiced authority.

"Valeri Smith," replied the hotel man.

"Miss?"

"Yes. At least that is how she registered."

"And when might that have been?"

"Yesterday evening, around seven." Forbes squirmed nervously.

"Have you seen her before, Mr. Forbes?"

"No...well, I mean...this wasn't her first time to stay at the hotel. Yes, I've seen her before."

"But you were not acquainted with her?"

"No."

"Do you know anybody who was?"

"No, I don't."

The lieutenant gave him a searching look "Is there any thing else you'd like to tell me?"

"No, except I don't see what you're making all the fuss about. The creature obviously took her own life."

"What makes you say that?"

"Well, for one thing, we had to break in this morning. Both doors to this room were bolted from the inside...and the transom. The window is almost a hundred feet off the ground—no ledges or balconies. I'm no detective, mam, but that adds up to suicide in any man's language."

"Yes, Mr. Forbes, I agree," Cathy Carruthers said sweetly, "you are not a detective. Because, you see, I am, and it is quite obvious to me that this woman was murdered."

Mark cast an enquiring glance at his superior He knew from past experience that this was no idle speculation.

"Now, perhaps you can tell me, Mr. Forbes, who was the first to find her?"

Forbes was visibly disconcerted. "One of the maids, I believe, a Mrs. Grebski."

"Is she in the hotel now?"

"Uh—yes." Forbes raised his eyes in an attitude of reflection. "Shall I send for her?"

"Please do. And, Mr. Forbes, before you go—" The lieutenant was standing by the door to the hall and she drew the man's attention to the light switch on the wall. It was the type with two flat surfaces that you push rather than flick, and on the lower OFF switch was a fingerprint so clearly visible that it seemed almost to have been put there intentionally.

"You will notice," the lieutenant told him, "that someone has left their calling card. That is, if you can remember with certainty whether or not anyone else has used this switch."

"Yes," Forbes said quickly, "I do—I mean, it was me. The light was on, so I turned it off. Force of habit, I guess."

"That was this morning when you found the girl?"

"Yes."

"Thank you, Mr. Forbes."

As the hotel man left, the lieutenant answered her assistant's unspoken query with an audacious wink, then with one blood-red fingernail, she pushed the ON surface of the switch and looked up at the broken fixture. The bulb did not respond.

"What do you make of that?"

"Must be a short in the fixture."

"Must be," agreed the Amazon absently.

Mark withdrew the bulb from its socket and tried it in the lamp on the night table. This time it lit up.

"Success," he said, but as he turned, he found himself to be alone in his conclusions, however illuminating. The lieutenant was already deeply engrossed in a new line of contemplation.

"Let us consider the dilemma of the doors," she mused aloud. There were two; one door opened out into the hall, the other to an adjoining room. The hall door, she noticed, had a night latch and the customary hotel night-chain, which now hung broken and useless from the doorjamb. The other door, which connected to room 806, had a common slide bolt with a projecting knob that fell, as it was moved forward, into a notched locking slot. There was also a locking slot at the other end of the bolt housing, which engaged the knob when the bolt was in the open position. The lieutenant tested the easy action of the bolt, then withdrew it and tried the door. It was apparently locked from the other side.

Mark, close at her elbow, had been running parallel with her observations until she stooped to retrieve a toothpick from the floor carpet, and here he lost contact in a flash of Amazonian leg.

"Interesting," mused the lieutenant, toothpick held twixt thumb and forefinger.

"Very," said Mark, with some ambiguity.

When she straightened, Forbes was standing in the hall doorway. He ushered in a middle-aged, nondescript sort of woman, in a blue thin-striped uniform.

"This is Mrs. Grebski, lieutenant. She was the one who found her."

"Thank you, Mr. Forbes." The lieutenant turned compelling eyes upon her assistant. "Mark, while I'm talking to Mrs. Grebski, would you endeavor to open this connecting door from the other side. Perhaps Mr. Forbes would assist you. I should like to have a look at that other room."

Sam Morton, Coroner and Chief Medical Examiner, M.C.P.D., took that precise moment to arrive, followed closely by photographers and lab-men. The lieutenant guided Mrs. Grebski to a spot by the window, out of the ensuing chaos.

"Mrs. Grebski, do you remember what time it was when you found her?"

Mrs. Grebski had the look of a frightened child.

"Yes, sir—ah—mam, 'bout quarter to eight, I'd say."

"What made you investigate so early?"

"804 had an early call, mam, I thought the room would be empty."

"I see. Now tell me what happened."

"I knocked first, mam, then used the pass key. The door wouldn't open but a few inches, because of the night-chain, but I could still see inside." She shuddered. "It was horrible."

"What did you do then?"

"I screamed," she said looking as though she intended to again, "then I went for Mr. Forbes."

"And Mr. Forbes broke the door in," the lieutenant filled in for her, "saw that she was long dead, and called us."

"That's right, mam."

"Mrs. Grebski, did you follow Mr. Forbes into the room?"

"No, mam, not likely."

"Did anyone?"

"Uh—no, mam."

"You're sure of that?"

"Yes, mam."

"Thank you, Mrs. Grebski, you may go."

As the maid stepped gingerly around the luckless Ms. Smith, on her way to the door, the Medical Examiner looked up to see the top half of Lieutenant Cathy Carruthers disappearing out the open window. She was prevented from disappearing entirely only by the tender balance of the remaining half (which he regarded with unprofessional interest) as it maneuvered her through an examination of the window's exterior, and an exquisite re-entry.

"Intriguing," she mused, regaining her lofty stature with a toss of her blonde head.

"Very," Sam Morton agreed, averting his eyes.

"Sam." She favored him with a disarming smile. "You've something to tell me?"

"Nothing you don't already know, lieutenant."

"Strangulation?"

"Yes."

"Can you pin the time down?"

"You want an educated guess?"

"In the absence of anything better, yes."

"I'd say—six to eight hours."

"Mmm—was the neck broken?"

"I think not."

"That was something I didn't know, Sam. Thank you."

Mark came through the connecting door just as Valeri Smith was being borne horizontally out the other. He found the lieutenant inspecting the contents of the dead woman's overnight bag. The bag looked as though it had been rifled.

"Has this been disturbed?" asked the lieutenant.

"Not prior to your arrival," Mr. Forbes volunteered from the doorway.

"And these?" She indicated some clothing that hung in a doorless alcove, serving as a clothes closet; a gaily patterned dress, a slip, and a three-quarter coat. The coat was beltless, but the leather trim on the collar matched the belt that had circled the pretty neck of Valeri Smith.

The hotel man shook his head. "Not to my knowledge," he said.

"Mr. Forbes," the lieutenant favored him with a long look, "I wonder if you would get me the name of the person, if any, who occupied room 806 last night."

"I already have that information, lieutenant," said Mark. "It was a Mr. Wilson Greaves, sales representative from out of town, in plastics, or so the register says; fiftyish, a hundred and fifty pounds, five-foot-six and bald as a billiard ball. Booked in at about 11 P.M. and left with the night owl."

"What time did the night owl leave?"

"The night clerk saw a man answering Greaves' description leave the hotel just after midnight, about 12:15. And, incidentally, both rooms were arranged-for a day ahead, simultaneously, by someone who identified herself as Greaves' secretary."

"Thank you, Mark." She projected a just reward. "Now let's have a look at this other room."

* * . *

In the open doorway, the lieutenant stopped to trace a barely distinguishable line with her fingertips, across the varnished surface of the doorjamb. There was an identical mark on the now accessible edge of the open door. By closing the door, she was able to bring the lines together. Both marks were the same approximate height as the bolt in 804.

"Has this room been cleaned yet, Mr. Forbes?"

"Not yet."

The bed showed no sign of having been slept in and there was no luggage, or clothing, or any sign of occupancy. A door key, stamped 806, was on the bureau.

"And the door to the hall, Mr. Forbes. Was it locked when you came through, just now?"

"Yes, it was. I used my pass key."

"Good. Mark, see if you can't find traces of burning in that metal wastebasket. I'll check the bathroom."

Under the lip of the toilet bowl, the lieutenant found several irregular pieces of ash residue. She was slipping them into a white envelope when Mark came in holding up a blackened hand.

"Somebody's burned something in there," he said, "but how did you know?"

"I didn't," she smiled, "but I do now."

She continued to poke around the room until a seascape above the bed caught her eye. It was slightly askew, and she straightened it. A half inch strip immediately below the picture was noticeably lighter than the surrounding wall.

"Mark," said the lieutenant, without a smile, "I want you to put out an all-points on Mr. Wilson Greaves. I'm afraid we shall have to detain that gentleman for questioning." She stopped on her way out the door, and turned, and as though on second thought, she added; "And Mr. Forbes, we shall want you as well."

"Me?—want me?" Forbes was livid. "For what?"

The lieutenant spoke softly, with a forced calm.

"The part you have played in this affair, Mr. Forbes, poses no mystery for me. Your bungling, obvious attempts to hide one crime, has implicated you in another. I am in doubt at this point, only, as to why."

Mark's look of amazement was paralleled by the show of utter disbelief on the face of the hotel manager, and he wondered if he would ever have enough answers of his own to withstand the initial impact of these oracular bombshells. But when the dust had settled, there were only questions, still. Before he could put voice to them, the Amazon was fast disappearing down the hall.

Lieutenant Cathy Carruthers sat atop her desk in the squad room, adorning her fingernails with a fresh coating of blood-red lacquer. Behind his own desk, Mark Swanson had propped his feet on an open drawer and was regarding his attractive colleague with mild chagrin.

"Okay," he said, "give—"

The lieutenant smiled, sphinx-like. "A simple matter of observation," she said lightly. She crossed one majestic leg over the other, contributing nothing to local jurisprudence.

"Out maneuvered again," muttered Mark.

"To begin with," began the lieutenant, "let's examine the unlikely premise that Valeri Smith committed suicide. Frankly, Mark, I thought it inconceivable that any woman (and a vain one, in particular—did you notice those pedicured toes?) would deliberately suffer the indignity of being found stark naked and, at the same time, so horribly visaged. Dead, yes; dead and naked, perhaps; repugnantly dead and/or naked, no. There was just no point in it. I thought it more likely she had worn a nightie, or a slip of some sort, that it was perhaps torn during a struggle, and subsequently removed from the scene, as not in keeping with the suicide idea."

"Mmm," said Mark.

"Then, again, it appeared to me most inconsistent, that a person, sufficiently disturbed as to contemplate the act of suicide, would switch on the television for a little viewing before hand. I'm more inclined to think that the television was used to cover the sounds of struggle, and whomever, after doing her in (so to speak), simply neglected to turn off the set."

"Logical," said Mark, "but hardly conclusive. Surely you had more to go on than that when you told Forbes we had a murderer on our hands."

"Not conclusive?" The lieutenant held up a red-tipped hand for inspection, her blonde head tilted appraisingly. "...to a man, perhaps. Honestly, Mark, sometimes the lack of insight in you men astounds me. But then, women are built so differently, aren't they?"

Mark conceded, silently and with approbation.

"Besides, it was physically impossible for Valeri Smith to have hanged herself from that chair."

"What? But I measured—"

"I know," said the lieutenant, beginning now to paint the nails on her other hand, "but only after the body had hung there for some time, and the leather belt that held her had been given time to stretch. Leather stretches frightfully, you know. And, if you remember, the light fixture was pulled down away from the ceiling, somewhat, which would tend to widen the gap still further—in as much as it was higher in its original position. Then, too, the weight of her body, if she had stood on the chair, would have depressed the upholstered seat by two or three inches. There just wasn't sufficient margin to accommodate any one of these factors, never mind all of them."

The lieutenant hung her nails up to dry, wrists limp, hands high.

"One more thing," she said, "there were pieces of well-trampled plaster that had broken away from the ceiling when the light fixture was pulled from its fastenings, littered over the floor below the body and the overturned chair, where the feet of Valeri Smith would not have stood (due to them being suspended in mid-air before the plaster had fallen), and where no other feet, save those of her hangman, could have stood, and then only prior to, or simultaneous with, the staging of that gruesome little charade, bolted doors and all, that subsequently greeted Mrs. Grebski, Mr. Forbes, and our unhappy selves, in that precise order. So you see, Mark, the suicide supposition would appear to have very little left to support it."

Mark lit a cigarette.

"If she didn't hang herself, then how do you suggest someone went about staging a private neck-tie party on the eighth floor of a busy hotel in the middle of the city? It seems to me—"

"I strongly suspect," the lieutenant put in serenely, "that she was hung there, by a person, or persons, yet unknown. Recall now, from your anatomical studies at the Police Academy: the relative strength of a woman's neck, in relation to her bodyweight is such, that even a short drop of this kind would normally break it. I say normally, because it is not inevitable; just probable. But Valeri Smith's neck was not broken; she died of strangulation. Not conclusive, mind, not in itself, but every substantiating clue serves to strengthen the premise as a whole. Don't you agree?"

Before Mark could respond, agreeably or otherwise, the telephone jangled with sudden alarm. The lieutenant tilted on her ample axis and reached for it, stretching over the desk top with the fluid grace of a panther.

This was no longer employment, Mark told himself; it was a form of entertainment.

"Lieutenant Carruthers here." She listened a moment, then said, "fine. Have them bring him up when they get in. And sergeant, would you send an escort for Forbes. Yes, we're holding him now. I'd like him here when we talk to Greaves."

The sound of the sergeant's voice crackled discordantly through the receiver, and with a show of agitation she held the instrument away from her ear. When she could get a word in, she said, "Sergeant, I'll sign it—when I come by the desk. Right—and while you're at it, see if you can chase up those reports from the coroner's office. No—and I still haven't heard from lab, or records—as you say, sergeant."

When she had replaced the instrument and regained her equilibrium, she said, "Men!"

Mark said. "So they've got Greaves."

"Yes, and I've got hunger pangs." She looked at her watch. "How about some lunch?"

"Thought you'd never ask."

"Let's try Lil Olys'—it's close, and it's quick."

"Match for the damage?"

"Uh-uh." The lieutenant shook her golden head.

"Dutch?"

"Dutch."

On the street, Cathy Carruthers walked tall and tempered at his side, with a naked animal stealth that made Mark astutely aware of the almost awesome intelligence and strength possessed by this amazing woman.

Seated across from Cathy Carruthers at Lil Olys' Cafeteria, Mark was aware that he was sheltering a callow sense of pride, a feeling of outright resentment, and a thin disguise of professional pedantry; pride, in his sometime-role of escort to the magnificent Amazon, resentment, in the endless turning of male heads, and, the inevitable ogling. To suppress any such activity, he knew, would require an exercise that would be tantamount to the total arrestment of crime itself.

He allowed his mind to wander these avenues for a time, until wild conjecture carried him into a nightmare of such outlandish fancy that he was happy, at length, to turn his thoughts back to the only somewhat less untenable complicacies surrounding the demise of Valeri Smith. With a hot corned beef sandwich under his belt and a cup of coffee warming his palate, Mark began to feel a little less like a student cadet at the police academy.

"Okay," he said with a sigh of resignation, "so Valeri Smith did not take her own life—then what explanation do you have for this business of the locked room?"

The lieutenant sipped thoughtfully on a glass of milk.

"Well, once we had ruled out the possibility of suicide, it followed categorically that someone had come and gone through one of the two locked doors, or an eighth-storey window. Of the three, the connecting door seemed to me the least formidable. That was where I found the toothpick, remember, directly beneath the bolt; which, incidentally, gave me my first clue as to how it was accomplished."

"Do tell," said Mark.

"If you recall, the bolt housing had a notched locking slot that engaged the projecting knob (by the simple expedient of gravity) in both the locked and the open position. It was to off-set this gravitational action that the toothpick, presumably, had been inserted between the bolt and the housing, thereby preventing the bolt from revolving and the projecting knob from dropping into the locking slot. This would permit the bolt, while still in the open position, to be drawn forward (by whatever means) without interception. Once released, the toothpick would simply fall to the floor."

"I'm with you, lieutenant. A common piece of string could have done it; one end tied to the knob on the bolt, the other passed around the end of the door. Then, with the door closed, the string could have been manipulated from 806."

"Exactly," said the lieutenant, adding impishly, "but then, how would you dispose of the string?"

"Yeah, how?"

"It puzzled me, too, until I spotted the seascape in 806. The painting had obviously been disturbed; taken down in fact, and the picture wire removed, then hurriedly replaced so that the frame rested higher on the wall than before. This, you remember, was not noticeable while the picture was askew, but only after I had straightened it, which was probably why it was overlooked. The wire, of course, made a perfect tool with which to draw the bolt; a wide, non-slip loop would easily have moved the bolt horizontally, then when slackened, would tend to spring away from the knob, allowing it to fall of its own accord into the locking slot. The wire could then be drawn back into the other room, and replaced. I suspect the end of the wire, twisted to effect the loop, was responsible for the light scratches on the edge of the door and the doorjamb."

"And I suspect you're right," said Mark. He followed her with unbidden eyes as she deserted her chair long enough to acquire a second glass of milk. He sighed. The Amazon in repose was disturbing enough; in motion, she was mesmeric.

"I will admit, though," she said, on resuming her seat, "I did not expect Greaves to be bald (as a billiard ball, you said, which was worst still). After all, Greaves had to be our prime suspect. It meant the hair we found in Valeri Smith's clenched fist could not have come from him; at least, not from his head. In view of this, I permitted myself the somewhat improbable supposition that Mr.Greaves was well haired below the neck, if not above it. Purely an assumption, you understand, but still, the hair sample did more closely resemble body hair than the scalp variety. And if it were so, (Greaves being our culprit) it would mean that he had not been fully clothed at the time of the murder. Then, when you consider that Miss Smith, too, had been scantily clad, if at all, there seemed little doubt they enjoyed a passing familiarity. As a matter of fact, it was possible— and to my thinking, even probable—that Valeri Smith and Wilson Greaves were involved in something of an affair, in the most lurid sense of the word. Their meeting last night, in those rooms, obviously had been no accident. We can safely assume, I'm sure, that the reservations had been made by the luckless Miss Smith, herself, and with the full knowledge and consent of our Mr. Greaves." The lieutenant knitted her brows. "But the relationship struck me as being most incongruous."

"How do you mean?"

"Well, for one thing, their ages weren't compatible. She just didn't seem the type, even dead, to become unselfishly involved with a man twice her years, and particularly one who appeared to have no physical attractiveness. Nor did the surreptitiousness of their meeting seem overly indicative of true love. To me, their intimacy suggested something more. Something—sinister."

"I smell a motive," said Mark.

"And well you might," said the lieutenant, "for it is my contention that Wilson Greaves was the victim of blackmail, that for whatever reason he met Miss Smith last night, he eventually recovered and subsequently destroyed, certain incriminating documents. From the disheveled state of her luggage and those traces of burning in 806, we can reasonably assume that he accomplished his purpose."

"Then why would he kill her?" asked Mark.

"Why, indeed."

At the front desk, the sergeant had a smile, a pen, and a dotted line for Lieutenant Carruthers. She accepted all three, graciously.

"You absent-minded-professor types are the bane of my life," he said. The lieutenant smiled, indulgently.

"Any word from the coroner?"

"Not yet, but the lab reports are on your desk, and if you stop in at records, I think they've got a couple of surprises for you."

"At this point," said Mark, "nothing would surprise me."

As the lieutenant moved off down the hall, the sergeant's eyes went with her. (Quixotically, Mark gave the sergeant a brief kangaroo hearing and sentenced him to life in purgatory.)

The records department harbored the smallest policeman on the Metropolitan Force, hired some years ago for his status rather than his stature, and whatever his name had been then, he had been labeled the Leprechaun by all and sundry ever since.

The lieutenant took the proffered brown manila file. "Anything of interest?"

"That's putting it mildly," said the leprechaun, only too pleased to share the fruits of his labors. "It seems that your Mr. Wilson Greaves is not Wilson Greaves at all, but Wayne P. Grayson, vice-president of Halton Mills, the Eastport Plastics Complex."

Mark whistled softly.

"And," said the little man, delighted at the affect of his revelations, "until some time last night, Mr. Grayson's private secretary was a cute little brunette by the name of Valeri Smith."

"This ties things up a bit," said Mark, then, with a look at his partner, he added, "or does it—?"

"Good work, Garfield," said the lieutenant to the little man behind the counter, apparently having done sufficient research of her own to ascertain his true appellation.

The leprechaun beamed. "No trouble at all, lieutenant."

Mark was less generous. "Is Garfield your first name," he asked with mock servility, "or your last?"

The leprechaun leveled a long malevolent look at Mark, and turned on his heel.

"Scheee—"

In the squad room, the lieutenant went over the records file in its entirety.

"Apparently Forbes was better acquainted with the late Miss Smith than he was prepared to say," she said. "According to this, he's been seen with her on a number of occasions." Then, with a sly smile, she added, "Garfield is his first name—it's on his report—G. Leprohn."

Mark laughed. "You mean you really didn't know?"

Cathy Carruthers shook her lovely head and burst into a fit of laughter. And, together, they guffawed loudly and long. Through tear-misted eyes, Mark shared a rare and precious liaison with his goddess. In an unguarded moment, it seemed, she had descended briefly, but with equivalence, to his own earthly level.

A sharp rap on the office door heralded the arrival on Wayne P. Grayson, alias Wilson Greaves. The uniformed policeman who announced him, shoved him into the room, then left immediately, closing the door behind him.

"Won't you sit down, Mr. Grayson?"

Grayson stood there looking like a fugitive from a Yul Brynner movie. He was an unpleasant little man, hairless from the neck up, except for a pair of bushy eyebrows that kept his already deep-set eyes in perpetual shadow.

Grayson addressed himself to Mark. "What's this all about? Nobody will tell me a thing."

Lieutenant Carruthers towered above him. "Mr. Grayson," she said, "please sit down."

Grayson looked about nervously, then lowered himself into a chair. He was visibly upset.

The lieutenant went to her desk and exchanged the records file she had been holding, for the folder containing the lab reports. Without a word, then, she began to circle the chair in which Grayson was seated, slowly, perusing the papers in the file. Her heels clicked with a hollow echo against the floor, each step seeming to heighten the little man's discomfiture. His eyes reached for her as she came from behind him, then followed her through the arc of his vision, until they lost her on the other side. Mark, watching him, saw no aesthetic favor in the dark, sunken eyes; only a brooding fear. He had seen the Amazon perform this little ritual before, unnerving her prey, and he never ceased to wonder at the effect of it.

"What is it you want of me?" Grayson was having some difficulty in keeping his voice steady.

The door opened, and the same policeman ushered in an anxious-looking Forbes. The hotel manager did not display the same self-assurance he had rendered earlier. To the lieutenant, he said: "I certainly hope you know what you're doing."

"Sadly enough, for you, Mr. Forbes," she said, pleasantly, "I do. Please be seated."

Mark ushered Forbes to a chair.

"I've just been reading about you, Mr. Forbes." said the lieutenant, indicating the file in her hand. "It seems the fingerprint on the lightswitch in room 804 was, in fact, yours."

"I already told you it was mine," said Forbes, uncertainly.

"So you did."

Forbes pulled nervously at his tie. "You've got the wrong man, lieutenant. I did not kill that woman."

"No, Mr. Forbes, you did not," said the lieutenant, "but you did hang her."

Mark raised his eyes in a sign of hopeless bewilderment. At this moment, as co-inquisitor, he felt not a little superfluous. He watched as the lieutenant seated herself on the edge of the desk and wondered, as he feigned a casual disinterest at the crossing of one Amazonian leg over the other, whether these diversionary tactics were altogether unintentional.

The lieutenant turned her attention to the little man. "Suppose you begin, Mr. Grayson, by telling us when you first became enamored of your secretary."

Grayson cast a furtive glance at Mark, then back to the lieutenant. But his hesitancy was short lived.

"I don't suppose there's much use in hiding anything, now."

"We already know what happened, Mr. Grayson. We only want your corroboration."

Grayson shut his eyes in weary resignation, and began to talk.

"Yes, I did get involved with Valeri Smith, lieutenant. It began about three weeks ago. They say there's no fool like an old fool, and I suppose I set out to prove it. She led me on until I actually believed she was genuinely interested in me. I know it must sound ridiculous, at my age, but last night was supposed to have been a—well, a sort of betrothal."

"It was Miss Smith, was it not," said the lieutenant, "who arranged for the rooms at the Westmore?"

"Yes."

"But it wasn't love you found there, was it, Mr. Grayson?" The lieutenant's voice had an omniscient ring. "It was avarice - and the threat of blackmail."

Grayson looked surprised, but he continued, undeterred.

"You must understand that I loved her, lieutenant, damn fool that I was—and I trusted her. She managed to lay her hands on documents that would reveal, with further investigation, a shortage in the books of almost $80,000. Administration is my responsibility, you see; my partner is in charge of production. It was my shortage alright, but I needed a little time—"

"The price of silence was too high?"

"It wasn't that, exactly," said Grayson. "I think I would almost have agreed to pay her off if it wasn't for the way she went about it. She made an utter fool of me. She told me she already had a lover, her partner in this blackmail routine. She called me repulsive, and loathsome—a little, ugly old man—"

The words, tumbling out so fast, appeared to choke him. "I didn't want to kill her—I didn't mean to—it was just that grinning, taunting mouth—God, what a fool I've been—"

Grayson began to sob, quietly—a sort of guttural hysteria.

"What was she wearing, Mr. Grayson, when you left her?"

"Wearing?"

"Yes, what did she have on?"

"A kind of negligee, I think.".

"You're not sure?"

"Yes, I'm sure. It was a negligee, of sorts."

"Pink?"

"Yes."

"And by bunching this garment up around her neck, you were able to strangle her with it?"

"Yes, yes—"

"Then what did you do?"

Grayson took some moments to compose himself.

"It wasn't until I had recovered the documents from her suitcase that I realized she was dead. I went to my own room where I burned the book entries in the waste basket, then flushed them down the toilet."

"Did you burn anything else?"

"No."

"What then?"

"I dressed, quickly, as quickly as I could, and I left the hotel."

"Do you remember what time it was?"

"I'm not certain," said Grayson, "shortly after twelve, I imagine."

"And Miss Smith?"

Grayson gave the lieutenant a look of perplexity.

"But I told you, lieutenant, she was dead—"

"How did you leave her?"

"She was on the bed—on her back."

Lieutenant Carruthers slipped off her perch on the desk and began to pace. "Don't you think it passing strange, Mr. Forbes, for a man to admit to murder, yet deny the inconsequential act of hanging the body to the ceiling?"

"Why ask me?" muttered Forbes. "You have all the answers."

"Even if his motive was to hide his crime, to escape detection—"

"I don't know what you're saying," cut in Grayson. "I've already told you what happened."

"You have, indeed, Mr. Grayson. But if you didn't hang the unfortunate Miss Smith by her neck—who did? And why?"

Grayson looked from one to the other, as though genuinely mystified by the entire conversation.

"You were seen leaving the hotel by two people, Mr. Grayson; one by chance (the night clerk), the other by design." The lieutenant looked squarely at Forbes. The hotel man said nothing.

"Let us suppose, Mr. Forbes, that you are Valeri Smith's mysterious lover and cohort (purely for the sake of discussion, you understand), and, on seeing Mr. Grayson leave the hotel, you beat a hasty path to room 804 to ascertain the success of your infamous scheme, to claim your share of the proceeds. You knock furtively on the door, but due to Miss Smith's unhappy estate, she is unable to respond. If the door is not locked, you simply walk in; a locked door, though, would require a key—your pass key, perhaps—but either way, you enter."

The lieutenant paused before the open window, her back to the three men, a silhouette of uncommon contour against the afternoon sun. To the world at large, she said: "No plan or counterplan had foreseen this contingency. Your first instinct is to put as much distance between you and your dead partner as possible, and so you leave, your mind dancing with the grim and sudden imminence of disaster.

"Precisely how long it took you to conclude you were in no apparent danger—providing, of course, that Valeri Smith had not disclosed your identity—I do not know; but I do know that it was at least five or six hours later, before you returned, having in the interim concocted a most ingenious, but nonetheless preposterous, hoax, which you were then preparing to execute. Sadly, it was ill-conceived, and had little chance of success from its very inception."

"This is ridiculous," said Forbes, "you've got no proof—"

"But Mr. Forbes, we are merely posing a supposition—Now, let us again assume that you are Miss Smith's accomplice. Armed with a scheme to divert the course of justice to your own ends, you re-enter room 804 and make a hurried appraisal of the death-scene. To cover the sounds of your activity, you select an all-night, FM channel on the television, ensuring its volume is loud enough to adequately camouflage your movements, yet not too loud so as to disturb the other guests. The torn and twisted negligee does not lend itself to your project, so you remove it and burn it, as best you can, in the toilet bowl in 806. This you do on the premise that the adjoining room will not be as closely investigated."

The lieutenant turned to Mark. "Some of the burned pieces I retrieved from the bowl were paper," she said in explanation, "and some were charred remnants of a pink nylon fabric—it's in the lab reports."

"Mmm," said Mark. He had been trying to envisage what Cathy Carruthers, the woman, would look like in a pink negligee, of sorts. Her interruption had been unpropitiously inopportune.

The lieutenant began to pace again, more quickly. "With the belt from Valeri Smith's coat, the end passed through the buckle-guard to fashion a slip-loop, and then attached to the light fixture, you are able to elevate her body sufficiently to allow the loop to pass over her head and tighten around her neck. You take great care, Mr. Forbes, to measure the distance carefully, from chair to toe, so that it will look as though she had taken her own life, but (tch, tch) you over-looked so many details. Most glaring, was the fact that Valeri Smith had been dead for at least four hours and rigor mortise had already begun to set in. This was evident by the way her limbs hung out away from her body, instead of perpendicularly. From this fact, alone, I have known from the moment I first set foot in room 804, that the entire scene was a grim and shallow burlesque."

The lieutenant stopped mid-floor and assumed a thoughtful pose, one hip thrust elegantly awry, a finger pressed to pursed lips. Mark guessed she went 38-25-39 under the sackcloth.

"If that light fixture was to give way under the weight of the body, Mr. Forbes, it would have done so almost immediately. I would guess that as the belt took the strain, the light flickered ominously, and you quickly switched it off at the wall to prevent a short circuit. The finger that pressed the switch, moist from your heinous toil, left a vivid telltale print. You see, Mr. Forbes, you would not have turned the light off at the time the body was discovered, as you said you did, because the light, having been broken earlier, was already off. That was a stupid lie."

"I must confess, though, that you carried on from there rather well. The locked room, though by no means novel, was quite tricky. I find it incongruous in the extreme that now, rather than extricate you, it will serve only to ensure your ultimate conviction."

"I hope you're prepared to prove all this?" Forbes' manner was one of enquiry rather than of affirmation.

"Have no illusion there, Mr. Forbes." To Mark, she said: "Two pertinent factors pointed to Mr. Forbes in the second half of this double-barreled felony—motive, and accessibility."

"Right," Mark agreed, "his pass key gave him accessibility, both coming and going. But what possible motive...?"

The lieutenant turned to Forbes, "It's inconceivable, isn't it, that any motive would induce a man to undertake so grim a labor. Motive? Extortion, what else?—a vice with which this gentleman is well acquainted. Forbes was the only person who knew, without any doubt, that Grayson had killed Valeri Smith. By hiding this fact from the police, Forbes would have saved Grayson's life, literally. He had visions of selling this same commodity back to Grayson, in install-ments—it was a blackmailer's dream."

Grayson spun on Forbes. "You swine," he said with vehemence. Then, to no one in particular, he whimpered; "God, I would have given my life for that girl."

The Amazon looked at Grayson. "You might yet," she said flatly.

The Santa Claus Killer

Originally published in *Mike Shane Mystery Magazine*, December 1981.

"LIEUTENANT, SOMEONE JUST KILLED SANTA CLAUS!"

Detective-Lieutenant Cathy Carruthers lifted her honey-blonde head and levelled quizzical blue eyes at the man who had come bursting into her office.

"What are you talking about?"

Detective-Sergeant Mark Swanson regarded his immediate superior with chagrin. He wondered if there was anything that could ripple that queenly calm.

"It's true," he persisted, "Santa Claus is dead."

The lieutenant smiled indulgently and proceeded to scatter piles of official-looking papers with her elbows, to make room in the center of her desk for a vial of blood-red nail polish. Mark watched in rapt frustration as she drew a red swath over the tip of an elegantly arched finger.

"That's like saying God is dead. Really, Mark—who would want to kill Santa Claus?"

Mark thought about it.

"Mrs. Claus?"

Cathy Carruthers favored her two i.c. with another disarming smile and carried on calmly adorning her nails.

"Sit down, Mark. Tell me about it."

Mark pursed his lips, sighed obeisantly, and lowered his rugged frame into a chair. Working with the "Amazon", as she was known to her burly colleagues in Homicide, demanded certain compromises that might have daunted a lesser man than Mark. It had taken him several months on the job to see beyond the stunning, six-foot, honey-haired female he had been assigned to as partner, but when he did, he discovered a remarkable individual, a true friend and a detective of rare sagacity. Watching her now, as she hung her freshly painted nails up to dry, wrists limp, her classic features inscrutably unperturbed, he felt a mild alarm at his growing attachment to this larger-than-life Amazonian goddess.

"You were saying?"

Mark yanked his mind back to the moment.

"Dispatch," he began, "just took a call from a Lloyd Drexler, security man at Martindew's Department Store. He said there's been a killing in that big display window on Central Avenue, the one they doll up every year to look like Santa's Workshop. You know, a bunch of dwarfs making toys and things for Christmas, and some guy in a red suit and white whiskers dressed up like Santa Claus. Well, that's one sad Santa that won't be going down any chimneys this Christmas—some one just choked the life out of him."

"Did they apprehend the killer?"

"That's the strange thing about it, lieutenant. It apparently happened while he was sitting in the window going Ho-Ho-Ho to a crowd of starry-eyed Christmas shoppers."

"And?"

"No one saw it happen."

"Hmm."

Mark recognized that contemplative "Hmm." The Amazon, he knew, loved nothing better than a puzzling mystery. Mark remembered having once used the word "unsolvable" in connection with a particularly abstruse murder case. She had been quick to admonish him. "No such thing," she had asserted. "If murder can be done, it can be solved." And solve it she did.

Mark scrambled up on his size twelves as the lieutenant suddenly shouldered a red leather purse and headed for the door. The purse matched her newly painted fingertips, he noticed (as a good officer should)—and her lipstick.

"Where to?" he asked.

"To find out who would want to kill Santa Claus on the very Eve of Christmas," she tossed back over her shoulder, "and why."

Christmas at Martindew's was advertised as a family affair. They had used the "family" motif from the beginning, back to thirty years ago when it was known as Martindew's General Store, and run mostly by family members. The business had flourished over the years, evolving rapidly into one of the largest departmentalized stores in the entire state. The seasonal window display, "Santa's Workshop", had grown with it, from a small nativity scene in an old storefront window, to an annual happening of almost legendary acclaim. Today, it was a major Christmas event in Metro, welcomed, and viewed with delight, by Santa fans of all ages.

Lieutenant Cathy Carruthers stood now in the center of Santa's Workshop and looked about her with coldly perceptive eyes. The window area, she observed, was about twenty feet wide, by maybe thirty, with a floor-to-ceiling plate glass window on one side that covered its entire length. The drapes were drawn now, but the whole exhibit was still operating at full tilt. It was a busy scene.

Toys were everywhere, toys of every make and mold, and a dozen look-alike elves, with big grinning heads and white gloved hands were still hammering, sawing, chiselling away at them, all in rhythm to a tinkling yuletide arrangement of Whistle While You Work. A huge pine Christmas tree stood in one corner, slowly turning, dazzling, with the glitter of a thousand ornaments and a magic mile of tinsel. And in the center of it all sat Santa, swaying gently in his automated rocker, with his glassy eyes staring vacantly ahead, and an uncharacteristic blush of purple in the once rosy hue of his cheeks.

"Has anything been touched?" The lieutenant directed her question to a uniformed police officer who, together with his partner, had been guarding the murder scene against well-meaning-bunglers and the just-plain-curious.

"No, sir—uh, mam—uh—"

The Amazon turned her back on the officer's confusion with an amused grin. "Wait outside, please."

When they were alone, she said, "Mark, it seems incomprehensible, does it not, that some one, or some thing, could have strangled the life out of our unhappy Santa—or whomever—and not been seen by someone, some one, in the crowd outside the window."

"Yeah, it's got me stumped."

"The most obvious suspects, of course, would be the elves—"

"Lieutenant," Mark's tone was disparaging, "how could a mechanical elf—?"

"Or someone dressed up like one?"

"Uh-hu," said Mark with skepticism, "and what about the thirty odd men, women and kids who were standing on the other side of that window, watching?"

"Yes," the lieutenant said quietly, as she moved to a spot behind the body. "As the late John Steinbeck might have said: 'Tis a puzzlement." She lifted the white hair at the nape of Santa's neck and exposed the sinister home-made garrote. It looked evil, Mark thought, even just lying idly there against the skin. It was fashioned of white nylon cord, with the replica of a small metal clothes-line tightener (also white) at one end, and a loop the size of a man's fist at the other. The cord, which was about four feet in length, dangled down behind the rocker and matched its tireless rhythm in a slow swinging arc.

"Recognize this, Mark?" The lieutenant rotated the small white "tightener" between an immaculately-lacquered thumb and forefinger. It was the cylindrical type, slightly narrowed at one end and with three tiny metal balls trapped inside. When a line was passed through it in one direction, from the narrow to the wide end, it moved freely; if the direction of travel was reversed, the cord was halted by the jamming of the metal balls in the narrow end of the cylinder.

"An effective clincher," Mark observed, "and available at almost any hardware store—but why so long a cord?" When he extended the length of nylon straight back from the rocker, it reached well into a small cluster of elves.

"Maybe that's your answer," said the lieutenant, and she drew his attention to the fact that only nine of the mechanical elves were animated. The three positioned directly behind Santa's chair wore happy grinning faces, but were otherwise non-productive in the Christmas effort of imaginary toy making.

"Lieutenant?" One of the uniformed officers had thrust his head through the partly open door. "There's a Lloyd Drexler here, wants to come in. Says he's in charge of store security."

"Let him in, officer."

A large man, six foot plus and built like a line backer, crammed his way through the door.

"Mark," The lieutenant spoke in quiet even tones to her colleague, but her eyes were on Drexler, "I'd like you to get the Medical Examiner down here, soon as possible. The Lab people, too, and the Photogs. We're going to need all the help we can get on this one. And Mark, have these two officers round up as many witnesses as they can find, anyone who was in front of that window during the past hour and a half." Then, as Mark turned to leave, "Mr. Drexler, I'm glad you're here, There are a few questions—"

"Yeah," the big man interrupted, "and I've got a few of my own. This here is my territory, and don't you forget it. And I don't want no guy in a monkey suit telling me where I can go and where I can't." He let his eyes travel up, then down, the lieutenant's imposing frame, "Now, I guess I got some dame giving me the I'm-in-charge routine."

The Amazon drew herself up to her full height. Her eyes had the glint of cold steel.

"Mr. Drexler. I am Detective-Lieutenant Cathy Carruthers, Metro Central, Eleventh Precinct. You can talk to me now, or not, as you wish. But kindly be advised that I am not intimidated by your supercilious, machoistic posturing. As a matter of fact, I'd be less them honest if I did not reveal to you that I find your behavior tiresome and churlish in the extreme, something more befitting a witless adolescent than a Martindew's store detective. Now—we can just as easily continue this conversation downtown, at headquarters, at my convenience, or we can resume where we left off a few moments ago. What is your choice?"

It was not possible for a man of Drexler's bulk to wilt, but he did slump a little.

"I—well—" he stammered, not knowing precisely how, or to what extent, he had been so imprudently squelched.

"Anyhow," he muttered, "there's not a whole lot I can tell you."

"Tell me this: are you acquainted with the victim?"

"Yeah. That's the man, himself. Nathan P. Martindew, President and owner of Martindew's Department Store."

The lieutenant registered her surprise. "What on earth would a man of that caliber be doing in a Santa Claus suit?"

"Nothing new. He takes an hour shift every day. Family tradition, or something. Says he's been doing it for thirty years."

"He took the same shift every day?"

"Yeah. Never failed. Nine to nine-fifty. Then the display closes down for ten minutes. Coffee break, a change of Santas. Goes on that way all day; every hour on the hour."

"Who takes over at ten, when Mr. Martindew leaves?"

"A couple of old guys take turns. They work out of the Display Department. Christmas extras. Nathan P. always hires them him-self—you know, doing the interviews, training them to Ho-Ho, like that—"

"One thing, Mr. Drexler, strikes me as rather strange."

"What's that?"

"With Nathan P. Martindew, himself, sitting here, dead—why isn't there more of a commotion in this place?"

"No one knows about it, that's why. If it wasn't for those two cops—"

The lieutenant cut him short. "I seem to recall, Mr. Drexler, that Nathan P. Martindew was somewhat incapacitated, confined to a wheel-chair, if I remember correctly."

"That's right. It was polio, or something. Anyway, he was pretty well paralyzed from the neck down. A lot of good all his money was to him. We had to wheel him in, then lift him from the wheel-chair to the rocker. The same again, in reverse, when his hour was up."

"I see. And weren't you the one who phoned the police?"

"Yes."

"And you also discovered the body?"

"Well, yes, I did. But Penny Lamb was right there with me. We closed the drapes, opened the door, and there he was, just like he is now, deader than a Christmas turkey."

"Where will I find this Penny Lamb?"

"Miss Penelope Lamb, if you don't mind."

The lieutenant turned to see a large heavy woman, equally as tall as herself but obviously not poured from the same classic mold, sharing the doorway with a frustrated police officer.

"Officer, let her in."

"As if he could stop me." said Penelope Lamb. She came bursting through the door like a Marine hitting the beach at Okinawa. She wore faded blue jeans and a matching denim shirt, both of which seemed to be stretched to the limit of their capacity.

"Please stay over here near the window, Miss Lamb," the lieutenant cautioned, "our people from HQ will not want anything disturbed."

"For all the good it'll do them."

"Now what makes you say that?"

"You tell me, lieutenant." Penelope Lamb pointed a plump finger at the defunct Santa Claus. "Old Nathan P. was in here all alone for fifty minutes, until Drexler and I came in together and found him dead. Even if someone else did come in here during that time, which they did not, it still remains that no less than thirty pairs of eyes were on Nathan P. every second of that time. I just don't see how it could have happened."

"Perhaps not, Miss Lamb, but happen, it did. And I intend to find out precisely how, and by whom. Now suppose you start by telling me where you were this morning, when Nathan P. Martindew first assumed his seat in the window."

"I was right here with him, lieutenant. It was Drexler and me who lifted him onto the rocker."

"And then?"

"Then we turned on the display machinery, opened the drapes, and left."

"That how you see it, Mr. Drexler?"

"Yeah. I was the one who opened the drapes. Penny switched on the rocker. She was still fussing with his beard, straightening his hat, you know, last minute touches—"

"But he was still visibly alive when you both had finally withdrawn from the display area?"

"Oh, yeah," said Drexler emphatically. "Nathan P. was an old dragon at the best of times, and a real stickler about starting on time. He made no bones about telling us to get outta there and get the show started. He was still nattering away at us when we closed the door on him."

"Miss Lamb," The lieutenant pursed her lips against an extended finger. "What is your particular function, here at the store?"

"You're standing in the middle of it, lieutenant." She swung her pudgy arm to take in the entire exhibit. "I'm assistant manager in Display. This whole show is our brain child—mine and Reggie Martin's."

"And who might Reggie Martin be?"

"He might be me, damn it. And tell this clown to keep his hands to himself."

A little man, with a head that looked too large for his body, suddenly appeared at the door. He was about four-foot zilch in his hush puppies, and no bigger than one of the elves that were still banging away at the toys in the window. He was dressed in jeans, like Penny Lamb, and a denim shirt that was open almost to his navel. A bronze medallion swung from a leather thong around his neck and shone like a small sun from the black jungle of hair on his little chest. A pair of white cotton gloves dangled from his back pocket. He was prevented from entering further into the room by the restraining arm of the law, one hand of which had seized him firmly by the scruff of his neck.

"Another one for you, lieutenant." The officer struggled valiantly to hold onto the little man who was apparently much stronger than his size would suggest.

"It's all right, officer. Let him go. But, please, no more."

Reggie Martin waddled in and took up a position near Penelope Lamb. He was about eye-level with her belt buckle. He had a ruddy, just-scrubbed look, like a reluctant little boy on his way to church on Sunday morning.

"And who might you be?" he said, looking skyward at the Amazon who towered above him like a giant gray sequoia.

"I'm Lieutenant Cathy Carruthers, Mr. Martin. And I am currently investigating the death of the unfortunate gentleman in the

Santa Claus costume. Is there anything you would like to tell me about it?"

"What is there to tell? He's dead, isn't he?"

"Yes, he's that all right." The lieutenant smiled thinly. "And where were you … this morning, when Mr Martindew took his place in the window?"

"I was in Display, right behind Miss Lamb and Drexler when they opened the drapes at nine."

"And when he was found dead?"

"I was still in Display, just where I was supposed to be."

"Do you two concur?" The lieutenant looked at Drexler, then at Penelope Lamb. They nodded their heads in acquiescence.

"I remember him there at nine," Drexler added reflectively, "but I can't say for sure he was there when we found the body."

"He was there," Penelope Lamb said unequivocally.

The lieutenant turned her attention back to the little man.

"What is your capacity, Mr. Martin, in the Display Department?"

"I'm the manager."

"I see. And the Santa Workshop exhibit is the creation solely of you, and Miss Lamb?"

"Yes."

"Has anyone else from Display been permitted to work on it?"

"No."

"Why not?"

"Because Penel—Miss Lamb and I have been doing it for years. No one else has ever worked on it. It's our baby, that's all."

"Yes, well—"

"This exhibit is not as superficial as it may at first appear, lieutenant." The little man sounded somewhat put out by the lieutenant's seeming indifference. "Take Santa's chair, for instance," he pointed with pride to the object in question, "it will not only rock on its pedestal, back and forth, but it will also move in a fifteen degree arc either side of center. If the mechanism is activated promptly on the hour, the rocker will complete one full arc to the right, and return, in exactly ten minutes. It will then automatically repeat the maneuver to the left. After a fifty minute shift (or ten complete arcs) the chair will end up precisely where it began, facing the crowd at the window. It requires a great deal of skill, lieutenant, to achieve that kind of precision."

"I'm sure it does."

The lieutenant dropped to one knee and ran her fingers appraisingly over the ornate pedestal on which the chair was perched. The switch that activated the rocker was at the back of the base and the mechanism itself was skillfully hidden behind a gayly colored facade, an elaborate rendering of fairyland fantasia around a horde of little elfin gargoyles that winked and grinned with the spirit of Christmas. The tiny grotesque heads were carved from solid wood and bolted securely to the base on all sides of the pedestal.

"I'm duly impressed," said the lieutenant with apparent sincerity.

"Thank you, lieutenant."

Their eyes met briefly on the same level before the Amazon resumed the perpendicular. "The elves, Mr. Martin," she said reflectively, "the twelve mechanical elves. They seem to bear a remarkable resemblance—"

"To me?" The little display manager moved obligingly to the group of three elves behind the Santa's chair. He donned the white gloves from his back pocket, assumed an elfin pose, and grinned. With a little make-up, he would have been indistinguishable from any one of them. "I'm the original, lieutenant. All the elves were patterned after me."

"Remarkable," said the lieutenant, but her voice suddenly took on a warm confiding quality. "Mr. Martin. I sense that you are inordinately disturbed about something, that you are not totally at ease with me. Are you able to tell me why?"

Reggie Martin tugged nervously at the bronze medallion and shifted his weight from one little foot to the other. He glanced hesitantly up at Penelope Lamb.

"Look, lieutenant, maybe there is something. But I think we should be talking about it up on the seventh floor, in Nathan's office."

"I don't understand."

"Reggie—" Penelope Lamb put a lot of concern into that one word.

"It's got to come sooner or later, Pen. No point in hiding it any longer now." He turned to the lieutenant. "It's not generally known around the store, but I'm not really Reggie Martin. What I mean is, Reggie Martin is a simple diminutive of my real name: Reginald Martindew. That dead Santa Claus, lieutenant, is my brother."

Lloyd Drexler's jaw dropped in silent disbelief. Penelope Lamb's rotund face was expressionless.

"Very well, Mr.—uh, Martindew." If the Amazon was surprised, she did not show it. "I see no reason why we should not accede to your request. I still have a few loose ends to see to down here, but we will all four of us reassemble on the seventh floor in say, fifteen minutes. But before—"

The lieutenant stopped abruptly in mid-sentence and looked up. The star at the top of the Christmas tree had suddenly burst into a series of brilliant, eye-blinding flashes. The lieutenant blinked as all eyes darted to the tree.

"What is that about?"

"Star of Bethlehem," Penelope Lamb said proudly. "It's new this year. People love it."

"I'm sure. How often does it happen?"

"Every hour, on the half hour, for a ten second duration," Miss Lamb explained, "I've seen people wait the better part of an hour just to see it come on."

"Well, we were fortunate indeed," The Amazon ventured with a dubious smile, "we got zapped without having to wait at all."

Lieutenant Cathy Carruthers and Sergeant Mark Swanson struggled through the main floor crush of Christmas shoppers toward the elevator lobby at the rear of the store. The frail familiar strains of Holy Night permeated the air, making something almost sacred out of the crass Christmas con game that had everybody clamoring over each other to give up their money. The elevators were taking off as fast as a bevy of young girls in abbreviated Santa costumes could cram them full. The lieutenant and Mark stood in line behind the others, waiting their turn.

"Well, lieutenant." Mark unbuttoned his coat and jammed his hands into his pants pockets. "What do you make of it?"

"Not much." The lieutenant panned an exasperated eye over the milling heads of the shoppers.

"I mean this Santa Claus business."

"Oh." She nudged her nose thoughtfully with a genteelly flexed knuckle. "I find it somewhat intriguing, to say the least."

"Well, I don't mind admitting, I'm stumped. There just isn't anyway it could have happened. Someone must be lying."

"Mark, how can you say that? We've just finished checking it out." The lieutenant's tone was more speculative than assertive. "The two relief Santas have corroborated the statements of Penelope Lamb and Lloyd Drexler, as well as that of the little guy, Reggie—whatever. I can't believe that everyone is lying. By the way," she added, "did you get that self-styled garrote to the Lab?"

"Yes I did,"

"Good." She turned eyes on Mark that seemed to be looking right through him. "I find it difficult to justify that loop, or hand-grip, at the end of the cord. And why was the cord of just sufficient length to reach into that grouping of elves behind the rocker?"

"It doesn't look too good for the elves, does it?" Mark grinned.

"Nothing about this case looks particularly good for the elves," The lieutenant replied soberly, as though there had been nothing facetious in his comment.

"Yeah, I see what you mean," Mark reflected. "According to three independent witnesses, Nathan P. was alive and well at nine o'clock, and in full view of a crowd of Christmas shoppers until ten minutes of ten, when Drexler and Penny Lamb drew the drapes and found him dead. The only company he had during that fifty minutes, were the twelve grinning, four-foot elves. But even so, lieutenant, what could they have done (assuming a mechanical elf could do anything) with all those people watching?"

"Yes," the lieutenant mused softly, "what?"

"This way, please."

One of the girls beckoned from the door of an elevator and they allowed themselves to be swept inside with a dozen other sardines. But Mark found no discomfort in being crammed into such close quarters with his enchanting partner. After the initial squirming, he found himself face to face with her, gazing breathlessly into those unbelievable blue eyes, just inches from his own.

"Hi," he said, with a crooked little grin.

"Hi, yourself."

She gave him a smile that promised to keep his fantasies flaming for a week.

The elevator clanked to a stop at the seventh floor with tummy-turning abruptness. An attractive black girl met them at the reception desk.

"Lieutenant Carruthers?" She addressed herself to Mark. The Amazon gave the girl a tolerant smile. She had long since resigned herself to this hesitancy on the part of some, to readily accept her, a woman, in what was generally regarded to be a male role. The girl conducted a brief woman-to-woman appraisal of the Amazon and said, "Follow me, please."

They trailed the black girl's engaging back through an immense, open room filled with desks, filing cabinets, rapidly clicking typewriters, and people. Everyone and everything seemed to be in a hectic state of regulated confusion. They zigzagged through it all to a row of offices on the far side where they were ushered through a door that read: Nathan P. Martindew, President.

The office was impressively spacious. A thick pile rug lay underfoot, and luxurious furnishings in soft leather and deep red walnut enriched the decor. A huge desk dominated the room, behind which, the new-born Reginald Martindew sat looking like a midget mushroom on a two-dollar pizza.

"Come in, lieutenant." The little man was effusive. "You know everyone, of course. Miss Lamb, Drexler, Miss Gayle (who has just escorted you from the elevator) and old faithful, himself, Elmer Sawatsky. Elmer has been with the firm for almost thirty years. He is our chief accountant."

"How do you do, lieutenant?"

A bespectacled, nondescript sort of man in his middle fifties offered a limp hand to the lieutenant. She took it briefly, nodded to the others, and folded her elegant form into one of the leather chairs. Mark took the chair beside her.

"Mr. Martindew." The lieutenant spoke directly at the man's head, which was all she could see of him above the polished surface of the desk. "Don't you feel that you might be jumping into your new role as president, somewhat precipitously, if not without a certain presumptuousness? After all, your own brother has just been killed—murdered, his body not yet cold."

"Presumptuous, lieutenant? Precipitous?" The new president had to raise his elbows to shoulder height to place his forearms on the desk. His little fingers toyed excitedly with the bronze medallion. "Hardly. I've waited years for this moment. The news of my brother's death this morning could not have come at a better time: Christmas Eve! How does that carol go now—Oh ti-idings of co-omfort and joy. You see, I make no illusions as to how I feel. Lieutenant, this promises to be the most momentous Christmas of my entire life."

"Reggie, not now." Penelope Lamb filled a leather chair to overflowing, a little to one side of the desk. "This is not the time," she pleaded.

"She's right, of course." Reginald Martindew tried several times to raise his head above the level of his hands. "My relationship with my brother, with my family, is undeniably a personal matter, and I would not normally discuss these things before the people who are presently in this room. But because of the way my brother died, and the circumstances that have preceded my rightful ascension to this chair today, the story, quite frankly, will be unrepressible. Every sordid detail will soon be splashed over newspapers, tabloids, and two-bit scandal sheets from here to Vladivostock. What would be the point in withholding anything at this juncture?"

"Then you won't mind," the lieutenant said as she settled back in the chair, "imparting some of those details you refer to, for our edification."

Reginald Martindew looked around the room, from one expressionless face to another, then shrugged his tiny shoulders.

"I was the oldest, the rightful heir. I had every appearance of a normal, healthy child, the first born, the pride of the Martindews, until it was noticed that I wasn't growing as rapidly as I should. By the time I was six, it was obvious that something was wrong. That was in the days before they knew too much about pituitary malfunctions which, of course, was my problem. Today, a series of natural-hormone injections would have remedied the situation, quite simply, and I would probably have grown eye-to-eye with your remarkable self, lieutenant."

All eyes turned momentarily to the lieutenant as though to see for themselves what Reggie might have grown eye-to-eye with, under more favorable circumstances.

"Nathan was born then, and I was shuttled off to one side, out of sight and mind. I never even knew my two younger sisters, whose twin births followed Nathan's by some eighteen months. As I grew older, the family law firm legally changed my name, and I was sent away with a modest, but livable, allowance. But, at the age of maturity, I returned, mortified at this rejection by the family, and by threatening to reveal my true identity, I was able to get a sizable increase in my allowance and a job for life, here at Martindews. What I did not know, at the time, was that only a few weeks prior to my re-appearance, the Martindew family had been touched by the hand of divine retribution (in my view, at least): Nathan, the favorite son, had been struck down by polio. The disease (acute anterior poliomyelitis, to be precise) left him totally devastated, and paralyzed from head to toe. Elmer, here, will attest to all that I have said, thus far."

Elmer nodded his nondescript head in agreement.

"Seven months ago," Reginald continued, "both my parents were killed in an automobile accident. The entire corporate estate, of course, went to Nathan, except for minor, non-voting stock allotments to my two sisters, who have since married and left Metro for sunnier climes. I tried to contest it—secretly—but I could not find a responsible law firm willing to risk the resultant pressures that would inevitably follow a suit taken against the highly influential Martindew administration. That is, until recently. Nathan, of course, was fully cognizant of what I was up to before he died, and did not actively oppose the action. Its ultimate success is ultra vires (as they say), inevitable. Simply a matter of time.

"How will Nathan's death affect your claim?"

"Not at all, really. Except that now I will inherit all—not half—of the Martindew corporate holdings."

"That could be a sizable motive," said the lieutenant softly, "for permanently removing your brother from the scene."

"Oh, come now, lieutenant. I was already a potential millionaire before Nathan was killed. Why would I risk all that, for money I could never hope to spend?"

"It's my job to examine every motive," the lieutenant replied. "Motives, like life itself, are sometimes obscure and irrational."

"What about the rest of these people?" Penelope Lamb rushed to Reggie's defense. "Take Drexler, there. His job was on the line. Nathan P. was going to fire him right after Christmas. Tried to get himself into bed with a young, pretty shoplifter, by promising to drop the charges. She went to the boss with it—"

Lloyd Drexler's face had turned the color of cranberry sauce.

"I don't have to sit here and listen to this," he fumed, "I'm not the only one with egg on my face. It ain't no secret that Miss Gayle here has been fraternizing with the office manager, and vice versa, apparently. How do we know old Nathan P. wasn't getting ready to dump him and her both? And Penny Lamb's relationship with Reggie wasn't all nip and tuck in the Display Department—he's been sharing her apartment for the better part of two years, that I know of. What they could've been cooking up together is anybody's guess. A regular old Peyton Place, ain't it, lieutenant?"

"Oh, my," said Elmer Sawatsky.

"And you, too, you old fraud." Drexler was not yet finished. "How do we know you aren't cooking the books and embezzling yourself up to those ice-cube eyeglasses you wear? Like they say, lieutenant, nobody's perfect."

Mark looked from face to face for the reaction to Drexler's outburst. Miss Gayle had turned a slightly lighter shade of black while remaining painfully aloof. Penny Lamb's flaccid face was an overt mask of indignation and anger, and Elmer Sawatsky squirmed in his chair as though involved in a private little struggle with himself for the courage to raise his hand to ask to leave the room. Only the little president seemed immune to the store detective's vindictive tirade. The face that peeked up from behind the enormous desk was wreathed in a tolerant, benefi-cent smile, a product, it would seem, of his new-found authority.

"Please. Gentlemen. Ladies." Reginald Martindew had now assumed a self-appointed role as mediator. "Let's not be carried away. The untimely death of my brother will touch on all of us, of course, one way or another. That is inevitable. But no one has yet been accused of anything. Have they? And I very much doubt that anyone will be. I would suggest that Lieutenant Carruthers is going to be hard put to tell us just how Nathan was murdered, much less by whom. Right, lieutenant?"

"Wrong." The lieutenant slowly uncoiled from the depths of the leather chair. She stood tall and silent for a moment, then paced out a small circle in the center of the room, as though modeling the latest thing from Frederick's, her exquisite body moving with the naked stealth and power of a jungle beast beneath the gray material of her suit. Mark knew a time of revelation was close at hand, and he wondered if he would ever become accustomed to the breath-robbing beauty and intelligence of this astounding woman.

The lieutenant stopped in front of Elmer Sawatsky. He seemed to pale a little behind his occular ice-cubes. Mr. Sawatsky," she said, not unkindly, "I cannot believe that you possess either the motive or the means—not to mention the fortitude—to cause the death of your late employer. If, in fact, you were "cooking the books" as Mr. Drexler had so groundlessly implied, it will soon come to light in the audit that will inevitably follow the death of Mr. Martindew. You may leave, Mr. Sawatsky, and I suggest you take Miss Gayle along with you."

The lieutenant turned to the young black with a condescending lift of her flawless brows.

"The allegations that your services to your immediate superior may not have ended with dictation, typing and filing, is of no concern to me in this investigation. You are an attractive young lady, Miss Gayle. It is my fervent hope that you will show better judgement in future when endeavoring to advance your career."

Miss Gayle hurried after the accountant and closed the door softly behind her. The lieutenant then turned to Mark.

"See that these other people are taken downtown, Mark, given their rights, and held."

Reginald Martindew's smile faded. Then the face behind the smile suddenly disappeared. A moment later, the little man came running out around the side of the desk, the bronze medallion flying in the breeze. He stopped about three feet from the lieutenant, his hands on his hips, looking up at her.

"Are you serious?" he choked. "You can't hold us. You don't have a damn thing to go on."

"I wouldn't be too sure of that."

"Are you accusing me of murder?"

"That," said the lieutenant, "could be a distinct possibility."

"You're making a big mistake, lady." He endeavored to convey with his tone of voice what a threatening posture had laughingly failed to achieve. "I'm not without influence now, you know."

"Nor, sir, am I."

Reginald Martindew's exasperation was suddenly more than he could rationally endure. He drew back a little foot and levelled it with irreverent spite against an hitherto sacrosanct Amazonian shin. "Damn you," he sputtered.

The Amazon winced, but made no sound as she calmly reached down and collared the little man with one well-groomed hand and lifted him, kicking and squirming, to shoulder height. "Cuff him," she said quietly to Mark, "and take him in."

Mark was no stranger to the occasional display of the Amazon's awesome strength and agility, but each new manifestation left him a little crushed, with yet another bruise to his hairy-chested ego. He took the weight of the midget president from her outstretched arm with a grunt of mild surprise, then answered her embarrassed grin with one of his own. "The Dragon Lady strikes again," he said with a whimsical little groan.

The Records Department embosomed the smallest policeman on the Metro Force, hired on the strength of his status rather than his stature. Few of his colleagues were actually aware of his legal name, Garfield Leprohn. Someone, somewhere, sometime, had labelled him the Leprechaun, and the name had stuck. Cathy Carruthers was leaning over the counter, talking to the Leprechaun when Mark caught up with her.

"It wouldn't take much to make this place into another Santa's Workshop," Mark observed wryly, "a saw here, a chisel there, some-one wearing white gloves and whistling—"

"If you don't mind," the Leprechaun scowled, "we're discussing official business."

The lieutenant contained her amusement behind a mask of pretended interest in the file on the counter.

"This simply confirms Martindew's sad little story," the lieutenant said in a tight voice. "There was certainly no love lost between him and his brother."

"There is one point of interest," said the Leprechaun, eager to share the results of his seldom appreciated labors, "Penelope Lamb has apparently been with the Martindew family for almost as long as Reginald. She was the daughter of a servant, a housekeeper. They knew each other as children."

"Interesting," said the lieutenant, "anything on Drexler?"

"Not much, except that he's been cited half a dozen times for the same kind of thing that was getting him into hot water at Martindew's."

"That figures," the lieutenant said matter-of-factly.

"The two relief Santas are just what they seem to be, innocent by-standers. And I haven't been able to come up with much, yet, on either Sawatsky or Gayle."

"Let me know when you do."

As they left, the lieutenant smiled her appreciation, and Mark went out whistling: Whistle While You Work—

Seated in her office, Lieutenant Cathy Carruthers went through the Records file again, in its entirety. As she closed the folder, Mark came in with another one just like it.

"The M.E.'s preliminary," he said, "The full report won't be available until after the autopsy."

"Is there anything in it?" the lieutenant asked as she accepted the unusually thin file.

"Precious little, lieutenant, and nothing we don't already know." Mark lowered his rugged frame into a chair. "Strangulation. Neck unbroken. No other marks. And a time of death that we've already come closer to ourselves."

The lieutenant flipped disparagingly through the half dozen or so pages. She looked up at Mark. "Did you establish the sequence I gave you to have the suspects brought in?"

"Yes. Officers Fisk and Mayhew have been alerted." He consulted his watch. "They should be here any minute."

"And what about the Lab report?"

"Whenever you're ready for it. I'll be right by the door."

"Good."

"But there won't be anything in it, lieutenant. After all, what can you say about four feet of nylon cord and a clothes-line tightener that had been rubbed smooth by the motion of the auto-mated rocker?"

"Not much," the lieutenant admitted with a grim sigh, "especially if it should happen to be around your own neck." She planted her elbows on the desk and cradled her beautiful face in the palms of her hands. "We don't have much to go on, do we?"

"Even our own private little dwarf from Records wasn't able to give us anything," Mark grunted. "Say—maybe he's in on it. Yeah, I can see it now: the Leprechaun, moonlighting as one of the twelve mechanical elves, picking up a couple of extra bucks for Christmas. He killed Santa Claus because he didn't like what he was going to get for Christmas—a pocket periscope for watch-ing parades, a reclining highchair, and the latest 8-track release of Short People—"

Cathy Carruthers tried unsuccessfully not to laugh at him. "Mark, don't you think you come down a little hard on the Leprechaun?"

"Temptation leaves me weak," Mark confided with mock inno-cence, "just can't help myself."

"I've noticed."

"And yet—" Mark's manner was suddenly, deadly serious. "That could be the answer."

"The Leprechaun did it?"

"One of the elves," Mark persisted, ignoring his senior partner's thinly veiled sarcasm, "maybe one of them was rigged."

The lieutenant settled back in her chair with a thoughtful sigh. She hooked a strand of spun gold from her forehead with a deftly curled third-finger and regarded her two i.c. with concern.

"I must confess, Mark, that your supposition is not without merit. However, I did have the elves checked out. There was nothing partic-ularly sinister about any one of them."

"But the three that stood directly behind Santa's rocker were not mechanized," Mark asserted. "What if some four-foot phony had dressed up like one of the elves, and taken its place in the window before Nathan P. had even been wheeled in?"

"Little Reggie?"

"Why not? Nobody would have known the difference. After all he was the original elf, wasn't he? He was the model for all the others— he said so, himself." Mark thoughtfully rubbed the back of his neck. "The only problem, of course, is how he could have done anything, anything, with all those people watching."

"Well, that might not have been as difficult as you think, Mark. It would be my guess, that if someone had stood behind the rocker, as you suggest, waiting for the right moment to tighten the noose on Santa's chubby neck, he would have done so at precisely nine-thirty."

"Why nine-thirty?"

"For two reasons. First, whomsoever would have to distract the attention of the Christmas shoppers who were all standing at the window, watching, and what better diversion could they have than the Star of Bethlehem? Every hour, on the half hour, remember? And I can personally attest to how successfully it would turn every eye to the tree, then leave them all blinded for several seconds after it had stopped flashing."

"Of course," Mark said excitedly, "that would have given him lots of time to—" His enthusiasm seemed to droop with sudden doubt. "What's the second reason?"

"The rocker," replied the lieutenant. "We were briefed on its mechanical precision by little Reggie himself – remember—and on its side-to-side movement in particular. Each fifteen-degree arc (according to Reggie) took exactly five minutes to complete. Therefore, thirty minutes after the rocker started moving (at nine o'clock) and six five-minute-fifteen-degree arcs later, the time would be precisely nine-thirty, and Santa Claus would be facing directly toward the window."

"So?"

"Don't you see? If an overt act was to take place behind the rocker, there would be less chance of being seen if the back of the victim were facing away from those who were watching at the window. The slightest movement, to either one side or the other, would only serve to diminish the cover. That factor, coupled with the precise timing of the Star of Bethlehem—"

"Right on, lieutenant." That's the only way it could have happened."

"Not necessarily."

"But you just said—"

"I said the supposition was possible, and it is, but from the facts we have, I don't see how Reginald Martindew qualifies as a credible suspect."

"How many four-foot suspects do we have?"

"Unfortunately, only one. And he was in the Display Department, according to witnesses, after the exhibit had been put in motion, and the door closed. He had no way of getting in there without being seen."

Mark turned his palms up. "Which puts us right back where we started," he muttered.

"Not really. Sometimes, in order to determine what is, one must first peel away the obfuscating illusion of what is not." She gnawed pensively at an asymmetrical fingernail. "The anatomy of a mystery, after all, Mark, was best exemplified twenty centuries ago, by Salome, in her celebrated Dance Of The Seven Veils."

Mark sighed. "—and the punch line?"

"Only when all the veils have been removed," she smiled, sphinx-like, "does one perceive the naked truth."

Mark lifted his eyes to the ceiling in a gesture of hopelessness. "Let's face it, lieutenant, the only "naked truth" we've managed to unveil, so far, is that nobody could have done it."

"Precisely," said the Amazon.

A sharp rap on the door signalled the arrival of Penelope Lamb. She stood in the doorway, bristling with indignation. Policewoman Fisk shoved her gently into the room, then left, closing the door softly behind her.

"Miss Lamb, please sit down."

"I don't like this, lieutenant." Penelope Lamb was visibly nervous. She squeezed herself into a captain's chair and inflated her heavy chest with a deep, tremulous intake of air.

"Miss Lamb, your friend and colleague, Reginald Martindew, will be with us momentarily, together with Mr. Drexler. But before they arrive, there is a question I would like to put to you."

"Hmmph." Penelope Lamb squirmed uncomfortably on the hard wooden chair.

"I realize that one can feel a certain misguided loyalty, or protectiveness, perhaps, to those with whom they work from day to day. Understandably. But I feel I must caution you that what we are presently involved in is not a simple misdemeanor. We are dealing here with premeditated murder. And in this state, the penalty for murder-one, is death. I want you to think about that, Miss Lamb. I want you to think about it, to remember it, and to govern yourself accordingly."

Penelope Lamb appeared to pale a little, but she said nothing.

"Now then." The lieutenant caught the nervously darting eyes and held them with her own. "I ask you straight out: did you conspire this morning, with any other person, in any way, to bring about the death of Nathan P. Martindew?"

"No. No, I did not."

"Are you certain of that?"

"Yes."

"You're not shielding anyone?"

"No."

"And you are presently under no threat?"

"—no."

The door rattled in its frame as Penelope Lamb mumbled her last denial, and an amused Officer Mayhew ushered in a much unamused Reginald Martindew. A moment later, Lloyd Drexler followed them into the room and quietly took a chair.

"Officer Mayhew, wait outside, please."

"I'm not saying a word," the little man sputtered as he shook loose from the policeman, "not one word, until my attorney gets here."

"That is your privilege, Mr. Martindew. I assume that you have already been permitted to call him?"

"Yes."

"Very well, then. We will simply wait for his arrival. Please sit down."

Sit up, Mark thought, would have been a more accurate invitation, as he watched Martindew's new president climb up into the only vacant chair. The over-sized head seemed to wobble precariously atop the little body.

"Don't tell them anything," he said to Penelope Lamb, who sat biting disconcertedly at her lower lip. "They don't have a leg to stand on."

As though to disprove the little man's statement, Lieutenant Carruthers stood up on (not one, but) two perfectly good legs and strode thoughtfully to the window. Mark watched expectantly from his chair by the door as she turned slowly to face Penelope Lamb. Her voice, when she spoke, was quiet and deliberate.

"I sincerely hope, Miss Lamb, that you are fully cognizant of your situation. However Nathan Martindew might have died, the fact remains that you were the last person to have contact with him."

"Don't listen to her, Pen. She's just trying to trap you. You don't have to—"

Penelope Lamb turned on the little man with sudden vehemence. "Shut up, Reggie! Just shut up!" Her face was flushed and beaded with perspiration. "I'm not talking; I'm listening—okay?"

"Sure, Pen—I didn't mean to—"

Mark could not suppress a smile as the elfin body suddenly cowered—then jerked awkwardly forward again. The leather thong that suspended the medallion around the little neck had inadvertently caught on the wooden arm of the chair. But Mark's smile slowly faded in the graphic hush that followed as all eyes turned to watch the tiny fingers untangle the offending snare. It seemed a silent eternity before the lieutenant finally spoke.

"Miss Lamb," she said calmly, her eyes still on Reggie's busy fingers, "I now must formally charge you with the murder of Nathan P. Martindew—"

* * * *

Penelope Lamb's face was the color of new snow.

"—you may remain silent if you wish—" As the lieutenant's monotone recitation continued, little Reggie squirmed in his chair like a recalcitrant child.

"Don't buy it, Pen. She's bluffing—"

"I told you to shut up, you little weasel." Penelope Lamb turned eyes on the lieutenant that were bright with fear. "How could I have killed him? He was still alive when I left the exhibit. Drexler, here, can prove it."

Lloyd Drexler vacantly nodded his head.

The door opened then, as though on signal, just wide enough to allow a uniformed arm to shove a brown file folder in at Mark. He accepted it with a nod, and closed the door as the arm withdrew.

"Lab report," he said, handing the folder over to the lieutenant. The self-styled garrote was coiled into a poly-bag and stapled to the front of the file.

"Recognize this?" The lieutenant detached the bag from the file, extracted the garrote, and tossed it across to Penelope Lamb. She intercepted it with nervous fingers, deflecting it back at the lieutenant as though it were white hot, or alive. "Damn you, lieutenant. I never saw that thing before."

Lieutenant Carruthers caught the snaking cord on one red-tipped finger and held it up for all to see. She read slowly from the open file in her other hand: "Dactylography: two discernible whorl-type impressions have been reimpressed from the smooth surface of the clothes-line tightener, one right thumbprint, one right index finger. Identification, as follows—" She looked searchingly at Penelope Lamb from behind an unruly fall of golden hair. "Miss Lamb, need I say more—?"

"Oh dear God!" Penelope Lamb slumped back in a dispirited heap. She looked at her little colleague with eyes that were glazed with fear and despair. "I told you it wouldn't work."

"No, Pen. No—"

Mark looked on in astonishment as the Amazon moved in swiftly, looming over her quarry like a cat with a mouse. "We know how you did it, Miss Lamb, can you tell us why?"

Penelope Lamb's pudgy face turned apprehensively from the lieutenant to Reggie, then back again. "I didn't want any part of it,

lieutenant. It wasn't my idea. Reggie set it up. All I did was—was—"
A sudden sob choked off the words. Tears welled up in her eyes.

The lieutenant stooped beside the woman's chair. "Miss Lamb,
what was your relationship with the Martindews?"

"My—my mother—" The big body began to jerk spasmodically
with a repressed sobbing. She blew her tears noisily into a tissue, and
began again. "Mr. Martindew (Reggie and Nathan's father) was—was
my father, too. My mother was housekeeper at the time, so—so it was
all hushed up, for obvious reasons. He promised my mother that he
would always look after me, even after his death. When—when my
mother died, there was no legal claim, but he kept his word. But then,
he—he died, and I went to see Nathan. Nathan just laughed at me.
Ca—called the whole story a shallow fraud—that I was just—just—"

"But you found a ready ally in Reggie?"

"Y—yes. Reggie promised that if I did what he wanted me to,
he—he would "deal" me into the Martindew fortune—legally, when
he became president. There was plenty for both of us, he—he said."

"That's preposterous." Reginald Martindew suddenly sprang to
his own defense. "Why would I want Nathan dead, lieutenant? I was
already assured more money, in half the estate, than I could ever
hope to spend."

The lieutenant sat back on the edge of the desk and crossed one
silken leg over the other. Mark noticed a small bruise on the left
ankle where little Reggie had vented his ire.

"The way I see it, Reginald Martindew, hate was your motive, not
greed. Hate, for the man who (in your mind, at any rate) had robbed
you of your heritage—your birthright. It had become, over the years,
a driving, waking obsession. There could be no rest for you, no peace
of mind, until your brother was dead and in his grave."

The little face on the too-big head was flushed with frustration. "I
hope you're prepared to prove all this."

"Miss Lamb?" The lieutenant's voice was suddenly as cold as a
winter wind. "Is it your intention to be a patsy to this man's appalling hatred, to shoulder all the blame, while he goes on his lucrative
way, free as a breeze? Or do you prefer to make a statement, to tell
the truth, and let the justice of your peers temper your punishment,
and his, in a more equitable manner?"

The withering look that Penelope Lamb levelled at Reginald Martindew seemed to preclude the need for an answer, and to reduce the little man's irate pomposity to the figment of a Christmas wish.

"I—I'll make a statement," she said.

When Officers Fisk and Mayhew had escorted Metro's most unlikely looking pair of felons from the room, the lieutenant regarded Drexler with an amused smile.

"What you said earlier, Mr Drexler, about Penelope Lamb and the late Reggie Martin "cooking something up together" has turned out to be strangely prophetic. But it wasn't quite what you had in mind, was it?"

The burly store detective rubbed his heavy jaw. "To tell you the truth, lieutenant, I don't really know what I had in mind. And I still don't know how Nathan P. was murdered."

"Well, it was actually quite simple," said the lieutenant as she resumed her seat behind the desk. "But it was only when we had established, unequivocally, that no one could have done it, that it became more obvious how someone had."

Mark grinned at Drexler. "Got another question?"

"Yeah, How was Nathan P. murdered?"

The lieutenant took their sarcasm in good humor. "Well, it seemed to me that if some one could not have done it, then, ipso facto, it had to have been some thing. And the people who were best qualified to rig that exhibit were, of course, Penelope Lamb and little Reggie. No one else was even permitted in there."

"But you said you had all the elves checked out," Mark reminded her, "and that they hadn't been tampered with."

"Nor had they. But to be perfectly candid with you, it wasn't until about ten minutes ago that I realized precisely how they had accomplished it. Remember, when little Reggie got his medallion caught on the arm of the captain's chair? It almost jerked his head off."

"That gave you the solution?"

"That was the solution. If the loop at the end of the four-foot nylon cord was not meant for the hand of an elf, then it must have been intended for something inanimate—some projection, perhaps, on the automated rocker."

"But—"

"Mr. Drexler, you attested to the fact that Penelope Lamb was the last one to leave the side of the victim. What appeared to you as "last minute fussing" was, in fact, the surreptitious fitting of the deadly garrote around poor Santa's neck. The whiskers and the hair effectively hid the device, which was also white, once it was in place. Then, when she stooped behind the pedestal to switch on the mechanism, she simply slipped the loop on the end of the nylon cord over one of the protruding gargoyles."

"But surely," Mark protested, "Nathan would have known that something was happening. He would have been noticeably upset—"

"And so he was. But, unfortunately, he could only move his head. Drexler, who was at the "drape switch" by the door, put it down to his usual feisty irascibility. The Whistle While You Work music would easily have drowned out his actual words. And the facial whiskers, which were created purposefully by the conspirators themselves, would have hidden any recognizable expression on the face of the victim, then, or later."

Drexler shook his head. "I still don't see—"

"The rocker, you will recall, moved from side to side, the pedestal did not. Once the loop was in place, the lateral movement of the rocker, combined with its jerking forward roll, would slowly tighten the garrote, cutting off the air supply to Santa's lungs. It is my guess, that he was dead by nine-o-five, after the first fifteen-degree arc of the rocker. Then, as the rocker slowly returned to its starting position, the cord would slacken off, and the loop would eventually fall away from the gargoyle, leaving it to dangle aimlessly behind the rocker. And that, of course, is precisely how we found it."

"Unbelieveable," said Drexler, "Penny Lamb and little Reggie." He rose uncertainly to his feet. "Well, anyway, it puts me in the clear. Am I free to go now, lieutenant?"

"Yes Mr. Drexler, you may go. But please keep yourself available. There'll be a preliminary hearing in a few days." When the store detective was half out the door, she added, "and Mr. Drexler, in the future, let us endeavor to keep our detective work separate from our sex life."

Drexler, with a red face, softly closed the door.

Mark looked to be thoughtfully preoccupied as his senior partner tugged on a pair of fur-trimmed mukluks, checked the contents of her purse, and reached for her coat. "Before you go, lieutenant," he said, "what was that ballyhoo about the fingerprints?"

Cathy Carruthers grinned. "I never did get around to saying whose they were, did I?"

"They were yours?"

"Uh-hu." She laughed. "Just a little Christmas humbug." She was half way across the room before she saw it. "What's that above the door?"

Mark had risen to his feet, blocking her exit. "Mistletoe," he said, without looking up. "It's a good thing Drexler didn't see it."

The Amazon moved in with a bedeviling smile. "Merry Christmas," she said.

Valentine for a Dead Lady

Originally published in *Mike Shane Mystery Magazine*, March 1982.

SHE LAY FACE DOWN IN THE POOL, HER BLONDE HAIR splayed out over the water like drifting seaweed. She seemed to dangle there like a puppet, her shoulders floating high in the water as though buoyed by an invisible bubble, her shapely hips and limbs undulating limply below the surface. It was not until she had been taken from the water, and stretched out on her back at pool-side, could it be seen the way she had died. Her once pretty face, now blue-lipped and mottled, had been run through with an arrow, the feathered end of the long shaft still protruding grotesquely from the center of her forehead.

The pool stood back about a hundred and fifty feet from the open end of the "U"-shaped ranch house, where the owners of Conklin Ranch had resided in comfort and conflict for half a century. A roofed-over patio filled in the "U" and a column of lofty poplars rose out of the green carpet of the grass to encircle the expansive grounds like silent sentinels. Beyond the trees, on three sides, the flat lands stretched away into gently rolling hills, their distant crests dotted with grazing cattle. And to the north, a scant five miles from the towering timber gates to the Conklin properties, Metro's concrete jungle sprawled over the unsuspecting horizon like a malignant cancer. The sun was already high in the heavens as a large, weathered-looking man in western attire stood waiting beside the dead woman, watching the approach across the lawn of two imposing figures.

One, a woman, was a striking six-foot Amazonian beauty with hair the color of ripe wheat. She moved with the effortlessness of a jungle cat, and even from a distance, the subtle power and grace of the body that moved beneath the camouflage of the brief gray suit was clearly manifest.

The other, a male, equally as tall, but thick-set and obviously well-muscled, walked in step beside her. He displayed a quiet self assurance that was evident even in the obfuscating shadow of his remarkable companion. As they drew near, Conklin addressed himself to the man.

"Lieutenant Carruthers?"

Detective-Sergeant Mark Swanson smiled indulgently and re-directed the query with a nod of his head to his attractive cohort.

"I'm Lieutenant Carruthers," the blonde beauty responded brightly. "Officially: Detective-Lieutenant Cathy Carruthers—Metro Central, Eleventh Precinct." She flashed her badge, then topped off the official dissertation with a dazzling smile. Mark knew that his senior partner was simply playing games. She no longer took offense at the hesitancy of some to accept her, a woman, in what had traditionally been a male role. He could not remember anyone, however, hesitating for long.

It had been the better part of a year, Mark recalled, since Cathy Carruthers had first invaded Homicide, Metro Central's last bastion of male chauvinism. She had met the challenge of her initiation with the femininity of a fire-breathing dragon, and had emerged miraculously unscathed some weeks later with the respect and somewhat reluctant admiration of her burly colleagues. They now called her the "Amazon", with affection, but showed no quarter in their good-natured taunting of Mark Swanson, her self-appointed and trusted side-kick.

"You must be Mr. Conklin," Lieutenant Carruthers said now with practiced charm.

"Yes." Conklin looked to be discomfited more by her smile than the revelation of her authority.

"You are the owner and manager of the Conklin properties?"

"That's right."

"Are you acquainted with this unfortunate young lady, Mr. Conklin?"

"Yes, of course. That's Melody—Melody Slade. She's my sister."

"Then, perhaps, you can tell me what happened."

"I don't know what happened, lieutenant. The pool is visible from my suite in the west wing of the ranch house. "There," he pointed a leathery finger, "you can see it from here. I had just got back in from the south range when I noticed her from the window, floating face down in the water."

"When was this?"

Conklin looked at his watch. "About an hour ago. Say, 10:20? I phoned you people as soon as I saw the way she had died. She looked so strange, lieutenant, laying there like that, her head and limbs dangling under the water. My God, who would want to do this to Melody?"

"Did you see anyone else?"

"Yes, Crampton, the grounds man. He helped me get her out of the pool."

"Where is Crampton now?"

"I sent him after Slade. Stephen Slade, Melody's husband. I figured he'd probably be at the Country Club. That's his usual haunt."

As they talked, the lieutenant's discerning blue eyes had been probing the mirrored surface of the pool. She turned to her colleague. "Mark, there's something floating in the water—there, just below the surface. See if you can fish it out. And there's something else over there, in the corner at the shallow end."

Mark reached for a gaff-pole from a pool-side rack and pulled a deflated rubber air-mattress from the water. Then from the far side of the pool, he retrieved an archer's bow. The lieutenant inspected the bow first, balancing it with professional familiarity by the taut string on the tip of a finger.

"Mr. Conklin," she said at length, "who at Conklin Ranch is able to manipulate this weapon with any degree of accuracy?"

"Me, for one, lieutenant. And Melody, there. We are both experienced archers. But we never thought of it as a weapon."

"Anyone else?"

"Not that I am aware of."

"Well, that seems to narrow things down a bit, doesn't it?" She regarded him intently from behind an unruly fall of golden hair.

"Now see here, lieutenant, if you think I had anything to do with this ghastly business, you're sadly mistaken. Why, in God's name, would I want to kill my own sister?"

Mark was not surprised when the lieutenant chose to quietly ignore the man's question and to center her attention on the bikini clad figure of the victim. She had been a lovely young woman, in her late twenties perhaps, with a good body that was evenly tanned from long leisurely hours under the sun.

"Mr. Conklin," the lieutenant said idly, "did you get along well with you sister?"

"Yes. She was devoted to me, and I to her."

"Did she also have a financial interest in the Conklin properties?"

"Yes. We are—were the only surviving family. We had equal interest in the estate."

"—until now."

"Now, look here, lieutenant—"

The rancher broke off as Cathy Carruthers suddenly dropped to one knee beside the body. In so doing, she inadvertently flashed a length of silken thigh that required no official dissertation to be recognized or appreciated.

"Look at this, Mark." The lieutenant had turned the impaled head to one side and drawn a red-tipped finger along a slight abrasion on the side of the neck.

"I'm looking," he muttered, with some ambiguity, but his eyes dutifully followed the path of her fingers as she cleared back some of the blonde hair that had matted behind the skull. The rounded tip of the arrow, now exposed, jutted out a full inch beyond the scalp. He noticed, too, with a slight flip of his stomach, that a certain amount of interior matter had come through with the arrow, although there appeared to have been little or no bleeding.

"It would require a well placed arrow to achieve that kind of penetration, wouldn't you say, Mr. Conklin?"

"Yes," Conklin agreed, "it would."

"And from relatively close range, with this weight of bow. Say—fifty feet. Seventy-five, maybe—at the outside."

"I'd say that."

"That distance would have put the bowman (or bow person) well out in the open, away from the cover of the house. Not the ideal site from which to launch an arrow with any semblance of stealth. The entire area between the pool and the patio is clearly visible from both wings of the ranch house. A rare and puzzling speculation, I must say." Mark looked on with interest as the lieutenant thrust out one supple hip and assumed an archer's pose before the rancher; one arm extended, the other drawn back as she sighted down an imaginary arrow. "It would almost suggest that Melody Slade had stood willingly beside the pool, face to face with her murderer, the very fiend who unleashed that deadly dart."

She let the arrow fly. "Ziiip!"

"Uh—yeah." Conklin had flinched at the release of the invisible arrow and tried now to cover his embarrassment. "I see what you mean."

"But still, if it was someone she knew, and trusted—"

The lieutenant's words drew some color to Conklin's weathered cheeks, but the man did not respond.

"Have you ever hunted with a bow and arrow, Mr. Conklin?"

"No, I damn well haven't."

"Well, I have, sir. I have no hesitancy in stating that I am an accomplished toxophilite of no mean ability. And you can take my word for this: the skull is an extremely resilient part of the human anatomy, especially at the point where this particular arrow made entry. The trajectory of the arrow in flight would have to be shallow indeed, in order to strike the surface of the skull at precisely the right angle. And I do mean right angle. Otherwise it would tend to deflect, to ricochet off the malleable bone structure and, at best, to achieve a minimal, angular penetration. As an experienced archer, Mr. Conklin, would you agree with those observations?"

"With all due respect, lieutenant, you're speculating in an area of which I know little or nothing. I—"

Mark Swanson looked on with some amusement as the Amazon again ignored the rancher in mid-sentence. It was a deliberate ploy, of course, to throw the man off balance, to get him to reveal something in anger that he would ordinarily have sufficient composure to withhold from her. But Conklin, though clearly annoyed, remained silent.

The lieutenant, engrossed now in an inch-by-inch search through the folds of the deflated air-mattress, absently fingered a screw valve that appeared to have loosened, then suddenly straightened with an I-thought-so smile as she poked an immaculately-lacquered finger through a small hole in the pillow end of the mattress. Her finger probed the hole, then emerged through the material on the other side.

"In one side and out the other," she said matter-of-factly, "just like the hole in the head of our unhappy sunbather. By the way, Mark, do you know what day this is?"

"Yeah, Saturday. February 14th."

"That's a man for you." She curled a crimson lip and arched the eyebrow nearest to him. "It's also St. Valentine's day. A little ironic, don't you think?"

"I forgot to send you a Valentine?"

The Amazon smiled patiently. "Don't you find it something of an irony that Melody Szlade should receive the original Valentine—imagine, an arrow—delivered by Cupid, himself, and right on St. Valentine's day?"

"Yeah, some Cupid—and some Valentine." Mark made an appropriate grimace. "But I guess it is kind of ironic, when you put it like that."

"Especially," the Amazon parleyed, delivering her coupe de grace with a bedeviling smile, "when you consider that the lady was dead when she received it."

"Huh?"

The two men gaped at her, then at each other. But before they could speak, she had given Mark an esoteric wink and was moving off across the lawn toward the ranch house, where a number of police vehicles had drawn up with lights flashing. Mark regarded the familiar contours of her receding silhouette with a blend of affection and chagrin. He wondered if he would ever become accustomed to these oracular broadsides—so casually expounded. And he knew from his relatively brief experience with this astonishing woman, that her startling comment would be anything but idle speculation.

Mark watched Conklin take off after the lieutenant as the various police teams began to converge on the pool area to perform their specialized functions. The Medical Examiner was the last to arrive.

"What've we got this time, Mark?"

"You're looking at it, Sam."

"Sonofagun." It took something bizarre to get a reaction out of Sam Morton.

"The lieutenant figures she was dead before Cupid delivered the arrow," Mark proffered.

"That so?" The M.E. emitted a disparaging grunt as he bent over the body. "You still teamed up with the Amazon?"

"Yeah."

"Might have known. That lady's sure got an uncanny eye for detail. Anything else?"

"You tell us." Mark had turned and was heading for the ranch house "And before you move her out," he called back over his shoulder, "you better have the lab dust that arrow."

"Gotcha."

The lieutenant was in the main central room of the ranch house when Mark caught up with her. Here, the Conklin money was clearly visible. The room was immense. From the high, vaulted, heavily-beamed ceiling to the mammoth fieldstone fireplace that claimed the entire north wall, it was the epitome of rustic luxury. The furnishings, like the room, were large and sumptuous, a pastoral fantasy of swirling wood-grains and soft, richly-scented leathers. Mark moved gingerly over the deep, sculptured carpet to where the lieutenant stood with Conklin, talking to a somewhat pallid, dapper-looking man with sleek black hair and a thin moustache.

"Mr. Slade," the lieutenant was saying, "do you think you can recall the precise time you left the ranch house this morning?"

"Around nine, I'd say." There was a thin thread of antagonism in the man's voice. "Melody was still in the pool. We left together, Conklin and I."

"Well, not quite together," Conklin put in quickly. "We left the patio at the same time, but your car was still in the driveway when I drove out."

Slade shrugged his thin shoulders.

"Then you were the last to leave, Mr. Slade, except, of course, for your wife."

"Looks that way."

"Were there no servants in the house?"

"No," Conklin volunteered. "Mrs. McInnes had set up a buffet breakfast on the patio, then left for the local Farmer's Market. I don't believe she has returned even yet." He lifted his eyes in a gesture of pained forbearance. "Her penchant for thrift is something we endure, rather than encourage."

"I take it that Mrs. McInnes is the housekeeper."

"Yes."

"Which means then, there were only three of you for breakfast. You two, and Melody."

"And Helen," said Slade.

"Helen?"

"Helen Mundy." Slade stroked his pencil-lined moustache. "She's my wife's physiotherapist. Melody was a health freak, lieutenant— you know, organic foods, yoga, massage, and now (believe it or not) pool therapy."

"I see. And when did Miss Mundy arrive?"

"She lives in. She has her own rooms in the east wing—just down the hall from ours."

"Yeah," said Conklin with a derisive curl of his lip, "real cozy like."

Slade's reaction was instantaneous. "Why don't you go milk a cow or something?" he spat out.

Conklin ignored this sudden hostility. "Helen and Melody were the first ones down," he said to the lieutenant. "They were in the middle of some kind of therapy session, splashing about in the pool, while Slade and I were having breakfast. Helen was also the first one to leave. Melody was on the air mattress in the pool, sunning herself, and we were still swilling coffee on the patio when she pulled out of the driveway."

"And where was Crampton during this time?"

"I sent him on an errand," Slade mumbled. He seemed to be in something of a sulk. "I didn't see him again until he came looking for me, after Melody was—killed."

"Was that before, or after breakfast?"

"Lieutenant?"

"The errand. When did Slade leave on the errand?"

"Oh—just before breakfast, before I came out on the patio."

"Stephen!"

An attractive young woman had suddenly appeared in the doorway. She wore a chalk white tennis costume that set off her trim figure with stunning effect and gave sharp contrast to a head of beautiful black hair that tumbled loosely about her shoulders. Her voice was on the quiet side of panic. "What happened? Why are the police—?"

Slade went to her quickly and took her hands in his own. "It's Melody, Helen. There's been an—an accident."

"Accident?"

"Melody's been shot. She's—dead."

"Oh dear God." Helen Mundy sunk deeply into one of the huge leather chairs. Her face had paled under a look of utter bewilderment. "Sh—shot?"

"With an arrow," Conklin added. "She must have died instantly."

Slade jerked his head up to stare open-mouthed at Conklin. Then at lieutenant Carruthers. His face was a veritable question mark. "Have they taken her away yet, lieutenant?"

The lieutenant glanced at Mark.

"Not yet," Mark said.

Slade headed for the door. "I've got to see her," he muttered, as though suddenly, inexplicably shaken by the full realization of her death. "I—I've got to see her." As he swept out of the room, Mark made a move to follow, but in response to an almost imperceptible tilt of the lieutenant's golden head, he held his ground.

"Mr. Conklin." Cathy Carruthers turned to the rancher with a condolent smile. "Miss Mundy appears to be somewhat shaken at the moment. Perhaps while she pulls herself together, you wouldn't mind showing the sergeant and me over the rest of the house. I'd like to start with Slade's east wing suite, then Miss Mundy's rooms."

"If you insist," the rancher grunted. Courtesy was apparently not a priority item on Conklin's list of things-to-do-today.

"And Mark." The lieutenant drew her colleague toward the door that opened out onto the patio. "Have a police woman see to Miss Mundy here, then assign an officer to go after Slade. I want him back here when we return. And, yes, we'd better have a team to give us a hand on our tour of inspection."

"Right, lieutenant."

As Mark left the room, the lieutenant motioned Conklin to one side, out of hearing. "You made an inference a while back, Mr. Conklin, about Mr. Slade and Miss Mundy. Would you kindly elaborate now, for my benefit?"

"Well," the rancher glanced uncertainly toward the girl, "it's no secret, damn it. Not anymore. Even Melody knew what was going on."

"And she still kept the girl in her employ?"

"Why not? If it wasn't Helen, it would be someone else. This way, Melody probably felt she could keep an eye on them."

"There was no bad feeling between them?"

"I didn't say that. Melody just seemed to keep things under control. In fact, they were quietly going at it this morning, when I came down to breakfast. Melody was threatening to tell Slade something she had found out about her—something from Helen's past."

"Did she?"

"No. The little creep wasn't down yet, and they had already left for the pool when he finally did show."

"What was it, that Melody had on Miss Mundy?"

"I have no idea."

"Do you think their affair had any substance, Mr. Conklin?"

"Substance?"

"Were they genuinely in love with each other?"

"On Helen's side, possibly—but Stephen Slade has no more fidelity in his pagan soul than a range bull in a herd of heifers."

The rooms in the east wing were two microcosms of the main central lounge. But for the frilled canopy over the king-sized bed, and the flowered pattern in the drapes that hung on the floor-to-ceiling windows on the south wall, there was no feminine influence in evidence anywhere. Lieutenant Carruthers drew Conklin's attention to the obvious omission.

"My father," the rancher said in his explanation, "has been dead now about two years. The ranch house is a kind of moment to his memory. Melody and I agreed, soon after his death, to respect his wishes and maintain the house the way he originally designed it. The west wing, my side of the house, is virtually no different from this—except for a welcome lack of flowers and frills—"

At the window, Mark listened absently to Conklin history while looking out across the lawn toward the pool. He could see Melody Slade being borne away under a white sheet, the shaft of the arrow making a small tent at one end of the stretcher. And Slade, in the company of a uniformed policeman was walking slowly, head bent, back toward the house. Here and there, an officer poked about in the flower beds, or probed the loose soil at the base of the encircling trees. The entire grounds were under search for some small clue to the identity of the missing bowman.

The inspection of Slade's suite of rooms had turned up nothing of interest to the lieutenant, and so the entourage had moved in a body down an inside hall to Helen Mundy's quarters. Again, there was no feminine decor, but here there could be little doubt as to the identity of the attractive occupant. The odd piece of therapeutic equipment had been left haphazardly about on the floor, or stuffed carelessly into a closet, and tell-tale wisps of feminine attire created a kind of nylon jungle in the bathroom. And in the bedroom, a fashionable "cubic-foot" tote bag, made of clear polyethylene with a leather draw-string opening, had been tossed carelessly onto the counterpane. An assortment of massage oils, creams and emulsions lay strewn, half in and half out of the bag. The lieutenant ran her finger lightly along the leather thong.

"It's wet," she said. "Did she have this bag with her this morning?"

"Sure thing—it's part of her stock in trade," Conklin attested. "She's seldom without it."

* * * *

In the west wing, Conklin's side of the house, they discovered a rifle, a 30.30 lever-action Savage. One of the officers held it out, cradled in a handkerchief, to the lieutenant. She was standing in front of the window, looking thoughtfully out toward the pool. It was the same view that Mark had from the east wing only minutes before, but from a slightly different angle. It would make an unbelievably easy target, she mused, an unsuspecting sunbather, framed by the pool—

"Lieutenant?"

"Huh—?" Taken unawares, Mark noticed, her face could be as soft and ingenuous as that of a schoolgirl.

"It was in a gun case," the officer was saying, "closed, but not locked. It's been fired."

"I haven't used that gun in months." A flush of color had risen to Conklin's leathery cheeks.

"It's been recently fired."

"Not by me, damn it."

She handed the rifle back to the officer. "Have the Lab dust the entire case, as well as the gun. You'd better hurry before they leave. And officer, have the swimming pool drained immediately, and the entire pool area searched. We are now looking for an expended piece of lead."

"Yes, sir—uh, mam."

The lieutenant smoothed over the officer's confusion with an understanding smile before addressing the rancher. "Mr. Conklin, I'm afraid you'll have to come downtown with us. I'm sorry to inconvenience you this way, but we'll need a statement, you understand, as well as a paraffin test."

"Where? And a what?" Conklin's tone reflected his mounting irritation.

"Headquarters," the lieutenant replied patiently, "and a simple procedure to determine whether you have recently fired a gun."

"Save your candle wax for the power shortage, lieutenant." The big man was becoming increasingly more irate. "I shot a coyote this morning, no more than an hour'n'half ago, out on the south range. At least I shot at it."

"And the gun?"

"A Remmington 30.06. It's in my pick-up. I never go out there without it."

Mark nodded to the second officer, who immediately left to retrieve the Remmington from the truck. Seeing the officer go seemed to trigger Conklin. He suddenly exploded.

"Listen lady," He stood squarely in the center of the room, his hands on his hips and a look of ugly frustration on his face. He was plainly used to giving orders, not taking them. "I've had just about all of this I can handle," he seethed. "Are you sure you know what the hell you're doing? I thought lady cops were supposed to be out checking parking meters. So what're you doing here anyway? All this crap about guns, and paraffin, and draining swimming pools—It's obvious to anyone with half an eye that Melody died from an arrow through her brain, and I don't intend to stand around here while you mark time in a pair of men's shoes that are clearly three sizes too big for you." He spun to face Mark with the anger still boiling within him. "Now take this dumb broad outta here before I really lose my temper."

The lieutenant spoke softly to Mark. "Take him in," she said simply.

"Lady," Conklin fumed, "you're not taking me anywhere." The enraged rancher turned suddenly and headed for the open door. In two fluid strides the Amazon had moved up beside him. One flawlessly manicured hand grabbed the back of his collar, while the other fastened itself to the belt at his waist, and in one herculean swing, she had lifted the big man clear off his feet and slammed him face first into the panelled wall. With her superb body coiled like a steel spring, she held him there, three feet off the floor, while her wide-eyed two i.c. obligingly snapped on the cuffs.

"Male chauvinism is one thing," she said with an embarrassed little grin, "but, dumb broad—?" When she let the man go, he dropped like a worn-out winter benny that had missed a coat hook.

Mark picked up the dazed rancher and steered him through the door. He stopped on the threshold and turned to look back at his senior partner. Mark had seen the Amazon in action before, but each new manifestation of the awesome strength and agility of this astounding woman never failed to shake him. She returned his haunted gaze with a look of sublime innocence and a dimpled smile that would have melted the heart of a hangman.

* * * *

Stephen Slade and Helen Mundy were sharing an overstuffed leather couch in the main central lounge when Mark Swanson and Lieutenant Carruthers returned to the capacious room. A uniformed police officer was standing just inside the door.

"Mr. Slade," the lieutenant said affably. "I regret that I must ask you to accompany us to Headquarters. We'll need you, too, Miss Mundy."

If the alleged lovers were upset with the lieutenant's request, it did not show. They both looked more confused and frightened, than annoyed.

"Miss Mundy." The lieutenant seemed to tower above them like the jolly gray giant. "Where was Mr. Conklin and Stephen Slade, when you left the ranch this morning?"

"They were on the patio, lieutenant."

"Did you see anyone else?"

"No, I don't think so—except Crampton."

"Crampton?"

"Yes, I passed him on the road. He was heading back toward the ranch."

"Lieutenant." Slade was having an impatient chew at his lower lip. "Is this going to take very long?"

"No, Mr. Slade. When you're all through downtown, you'll be driven back here. And I must ask you then, to remain within the residence. There will be guards posted."

"Guards?"

"Just routine procedure, Mr. Slade."

"How long is this going to go on?"

"We'll need you at H.Q. again, probably sometime tomorrow afternoon. The department will send a car for you."

"And then?"

"That should wrap it up."

"But—" Slade seemed to be searching for the right words. "What about Melody—the way she died?"

"Mr. Slade," the lieutenant said patiently, "I already know the way she died."

"Yes, of course. But—"

"But who killed her?" The Lieutenant's piercing gaze drifted slowly from one upturned face to the other before she answered her own question. "Let's just say that it wasn't Cupid."

It was a typical late Sunday morning at the Eleventh Precinct. The hectic weeklong hustle had slowed to a crawl, and a skeletal staff moved leisurely from one department to another, enjoying a welcome respite.

Lieutenant Cathy Carruthers sat with her back to her desk, a pair of tweezers in one hand, a mirror in the other, and a seeming disinterest in anything beyond maintaining an element of discipline in the eyebrow department. But reflected in the mirror, beyond the foreground image of one beautiful blue eye, she noticed Mark Swanson as he entered the main office. She watched him wave "Hi" at the duty sergeant, pick up the mail and a few call slips from the switchboard operator, then stroll nonchalantly toward her glass-partitioned office. The slight, involuntary brightening of that one blue eye betrayed the unspoken warmth of affection and the high esteem in which she held her chosen partner. She turned to face him as he entered.

"Anything interesting?"

Mark tossed half a dozen letters onto her desk. "I'll get the calls," he said with uncustomary curtness, "while you're checking out the mail." Then, to his partner's mild surprise, he turned on his heel and walked out to one of the empty desks in front of the office. Mark was on his third call when the lieutenant finally got to the letter on the bottom. He watched slyly as she opened it and drew out a heart-shaped card. The sudden smile she projected at him through the glass partition made the whole gag worthwhile. The card, with his own scribbled verse, read:

> Valentines are
>   Decidedly dumb,
>   But (broadly speaking)
>   You're sure a Hon.

The lieutenant made a gun out of her fingers, pointed it at Mark, and pulled the trigger. He was still savoring her wide happy grin, watching her slip the card into an inside pocket, when something in his peripheral vision made him look around. A little man, standing eye to eye with him, had stopped beside his desk.

Garfield Leprohn (the Leprechaun, as he was called by all and sundry) was Metro Central's shortest police officer. He was also head of the Records Department. His status on the force was commensurate with his ability, not his size, which was a happy circumstance for the Leprechaun, but he could never seem to escape the good-natured bantering of his life-size colleagues. Mark took a certain perverse pride in being one of his prime irritants.

"Well, Godzilla, what do you want?"

"It is not a question of what I want," the Leprechaun said, with all the dignity he could cram into his abbreviated stature. "I have the file on the Slade case, and I would like to discuss it with someone intelligent."

"Sure thing," said Mark, "it'll be a welcome change from talking to yourself." He got to his feet and ushered the little man into Lieutenant Carruthers' office.

"Garfield." The lieutenant's use of his given name was a courtesy the Leprechaun cherished. "I've been expecting you. Is that the Slade file?"

"Complete," he beamed. "I'd like to go over it with you."

"Please do."

"Very well then," Mark watched Garfield Leprohn make an irritating ceremony of selecting a chair, before he finally settled back with an open file and a closed mind. The Leprechaun was in his own, narrow, little data-gathering heaven, and he intended to make the most of it.

"Both Conklin and the dead woman," he began, "are (were, in the case of the victim) veritable pillars of society. There's not a blemish on either one of them, that is, if you can overlook Melody's recent, rather impetuous marriage. Slade, on the other hand, is a good-time Charlie from way back. He was implicated—but never charged—in a couple of bunko beefs in Seattle, about ten years ago. And that pretty well sets the stage for his whole penny-ante career. Always involved, but never convicted. His marriage to Melody was his third. One previous marriage ended in divorce (the first one) and the other in the wife's death. That was a drowning, where (once again) foul play was suspected, but never proven. Stephen Slade, lieutenant, is unquestionably one slippery customer."

The Leprechaun came up for air, and an encouraging smile from the Amazon. "Now we get to the good part," he said almost gleefully, "Helen Mundy." He treated them both to a sly, off-the-record leer. "She is not, as she claims, a bona fide physiotherapist. She is, however, a masseuse—of a kind. She learned her trade well in a massage parlor on the seamy side of Vancouver, where she was picked up for soliciting on three separate occasions. She was sprung each time by the same four-bit lawyer who was known to be on the payroll of a local pimp. That was more than two years ago. She seems to have made a valid effort, though, to play it straight ever since her last bust."

"That must have been what Melody had threatened to tell Slade," the lieutenant speculated.

"I don't know about that," the Leprechaun added, "but I do know that Melody had a shamus on the payroll. That fit in?"

"It does indeed. That was how she knew about Helen Mundy's lurid past."

The Leprechaun was delighted with the response he was getting. "Well then. Now for Crampton. Ellias J. Crampton, to be precise. He started working for the Conklins when he was twenty years old. He hired on when he first arrived in the Metro area, nineteen years ago, with nothing but torn underwear and broken finger nails." He snuck a quick peek to appraise the effect of his colorful prose. "He's had a few run-ins with the law over the years, but nothing serious. He's a lush. And, for what it's worth, Conklin senior was apparently devoted to him."

"Hmm. By the way, Mark." The lieutenant jotted something on a note pad. "Have we been able to locate that particular gentleman yet?"

"Yeah. Picked him up early this morning. He was holed up in some sleazy hotel on Slater Street, drunk as a skunk. They've been trying to sober him up ever since."

"Good." She turned her attention back to the Leprechaun. "Did you get anything on the disposition of the estate?"

"Sure did, lieutenant." The Leprechaun looked like a toy poodle that had just earned a pat on the head. Mark was almost tempted to look down and see if his tail was wagging. "There was a will, of course, left by the senior Conklin. His wife pre-deceased him, and he died himself approximately two years ago. The beneficiaries (Mervin and Melody) were given equal shares of the estate. Melody also had a will, in which she left her entire share of the property to her new husband, Stephen Slade. The Conklin lawyers intimated that Melody fully intended to change her bequest, which was made in temerarieta (while under delusion) immediately after her marriage. She just hadn't gotten around to it."

"Interesting," mused the lieutenant.

"Ellias J. Crampton was also included in the old man's will," the Leprechaun rambled on. "He was given a life-time annuity, calculated each year-end at one percent of the current book value of the estate (which, you understand, is much less than the market value) with a proviso entitling him to commute the annuity (to age seventy-five) should both the principal beneficiaries pre-decease him. Stephen Slade, by the way would not be considered a principal beneficiary."

"And the book value of the estate?"

The Leprechaun consulted his file. "In the neighborhood of eight-hundred thousand dollars."

"Some neighborhood," Mark muttered.

"Not," the Leprechaun pointed out, "when you consider that the market value would probably be over two million."

Mark emitted a low whistle and the lieutenant did a quick calculation on the note pad. "So, to sum it up," she said thoughtfully, "Melody's murder leaves Crampton with his eight thousand dollar annual stipend (which he had anyway), while Slade and Conklin stood to gain roughly a million dollars each."

"That's about it." The Leprechaun handed the file to the lieutenant with a look of smug satisfaction.

"And, of course, there's Helen Mundy." The lieutenant made a steeple of her fingers against her lips and tilted her beautiful head. "With Slade free to re-marry, she stood to acquire (as his spouse) a fifty percent share of half of a two million dollar property. It looks like motives and suspects are a dime a dozen this morning."

"Four suspects, maybe," said the Leprechaun smugly, thinking he was stating the obvious, "but only one of them is guilty."

"Quite the contrary," the Amazon added quietly. "The way I see it, only one of them is innocent."

The squad room was customarily a quiet place in the early hours of the afternoon. Sunday, February 15th, was no exception. It was this that had prompted lieutenant Carruthers to commandeer the room, her own office being too small to accommodate the four principal suspects in the still unresolved St. Valentine's Day murder.

There was a hush in the room. A policewoman and a male uniformed officer stood just inside the double doors. The lieutenant, at a desk on the narrow, room-wide podium, appeared to be totally engrossed in the files and reports that were spread before her. Sitting off to one side, Mark was thoughtfully searching the faces of the four unwilling guests. Just why, he was wondering, and by whose hand, had Melody Slade come to her grotesque and untimely end?

Sitting nearest to him, an unkempt and somewhat subdued Mervin Conklin showed the strain of spending the night as a guest of the city. He sat scowling at everything and nothing, tugging irritably at the tangles in his sun-bleached hair with thick stubby fingers.

Slade, though natty as ever, was cadaverously pale. His broody little eyes darted nervously about the room, looking like two lived-in maggot holes in a lump of gorgonzola.

If you could rely on appearance alone to establish guilt, Mark thought, Slade would be head of the list.

Between the two men, Helen Mundy sat stiffly on the edge of her chair, assiduously pressing out the wrinkles in a square of rumpled facial tissue. She seemed to have withdrawn into some dark inner refuge, her downcast eyes rivetted on the aimless activity in her lap.

The fourth guest, the illusive Ellias J. Crampton, had chosen a chair behind the other three. He was a gaunt and angular man, still in his work clothes, and bristling a two-day growth of beard on his thin square jaw. He appeared to be dozing, his skinny frame swaying mindlessly on its wooden perch, like a dry weed in the wind. And he looked to be more troubled by his unwilling withdrawal from the foggy world of the inebriate, than what was about to happen in the squad room.

"Lieutenant." It was Conklin who spoke. "I don't mean any disrespect," he said cautiously, "but I'd like to know just why I've been herded in here like a dogie at round-up. And why, may I ask, was I forced to spend last night in that crummy cell?"

Cathy Carruthers lifted her blonde head as the rancher spoke, her beautiful features inscrutably void of all expression. "Your brief detention, Mr. Conklin, was obviously self induced. Your impetuous behavior yesterday left us little choice. But I do otherwise agree with you. You have not been charged, and we no longer have any reason to detain you."

The lieutenant rose to her feet and picked up one of the files from the top of her desk. "You may go now, if you wish, Mr. Conklin. I had you brought here this afternoon because I thought you would be interested to know the final outcome of our investigation."

"You know who killed Melody?"

"Yes."

"Then why not just come out and say it? Why all the dramatics? Damn it, lieutenant, let the innocent people go."

The lieutenant gave him a condescending smile. "I have just done that, Mr. Conklin. The only innocent person in this room, is you."

"What the hell're you saying?" Crampton's bleary eyes jerked open. His head wobbled unsteadily atop a turkey-like neck. "I didn't kill nobody."

"No, Mr. Crampton, you did not. But you did attempt to divert the course of justice. And, strange as it may seem, even though all three of you are seriously implicated, there's not one of you who is totally aware of what happened."

"What's to be aware of?" Slade was visibly a frightened man. "Melody was killed by an arrow, and the only people who had access to the archery equipment was Melody herself, and Conklin."

"And Crampton," the rancher added.

Crampton's stomach took that moment to gurgle. He shrunk back in his chair, grinning sheepishly under his bushy brows. Mark could not restrain a smile.

The lieutenant raised her hand for attention and got it. To Mark, watching from the sidelines, it was an electrifying moment. She could be so authoritative and so incredibly beautiful at the same time, without depleting one from the other. He saw her straighten to her full stature, and sensed a subtle change in her mood. It was as though she had elected, then, to terminate the myth, and put living flesh and blood to Homicide's most controversial legend. And, in that instant, it seemed to Mark, she was the Amazon, myth and maiden alike.

"I think we had better begin," she said in a low decisive voice, "by dispelling any notion that Melody Slade was killed by a bow and arrow. She was not." She opened the file she had in her hand. "The report I have here, is from Ballistics. It confirms by an indisputable match-up, that an expended round we picked up yesterday afternoon in the bottom of the drained pool, came from the 30.30 Savage we found in Mr. Conklin's west wing suite."

Slade stirred uncomfortably in his chair. "Then how come Conklin's off the hook? It was his gun."

"Yes, and on top of that, his paraffin test was positive (as was yours)—nevertheless, he did not fire that rifle."

"How can you be so sure?"

"Well, for one thing, Mr. Slade, I find it difficult to accept that any man would be so transparently stupid as to commit a murder with his own gun, in his own room, and then leave the murder weapon in full view where it was certain to be found later by the police. On such a premise, we could almost logically expect to find his fingerprints conveniently left on the rifle. We did not."

"So what does that prove?" Slade pressed his point in desperation. "He probably wiped them off."

"Now why would he do that? His fingerprints were supposed to be there—it was his gun. No, Mr. Slade, it was not Mr. Conklin who wiped off that rifle. It was you. And even though you were otherwise very thorough, you'll be distressed to learn, I'm sure, that you overlooked one tell-tale surface."

"Will I, now?" Slade's attempt at bravado was not convincing.

"I'm referring to the cartridge case, Mr. Slade, that you inserted into the breach with thumb and forefinger, and subsequently forgot to remove."

A light seemed to flick on in Slade's head, to flare briefly in the hollow eye sockets, then slowly dim. "Damn," he said.

*   *   *   *

"Then it was Slade." Conklin almost tipped his chair over in his excitement. "Of course—it had to be him. He was the last one to see Melody alive." He swung to face his brother-in-law. "You murdering louse—"

"Mr. Conklin," the Amazon cut in sharply. "I will caution you only once to keep yourself under restraint." Mark had tensed instinctively, only to relax a moment later as the rancher reluctantly settled back in his chair. "It has been relatively obvious from the beginning, Mr. Conklin, even without the paraffin test and fingerprints, that Slade was the one who shot Melody. But even so, he is not your sister's murderer."

Conklin squirmed. "You mean he missed?"

"No. The bullet hit her all right. It passed through her head on a path identical to that of the arrow. The only reason he did not kill her was because Melody was already dead."

"Lieutenant." Some of yesterday's belligerence was beginning to threaten the rancher's Sunday behavior. "I chose to remain here to get some answers, not more riddles. If Slade didn't kill her, then who the hell did?"

"Think, Mr. Conklin, to when we first viewed your sister's body." She spoke quietly, as though she were mentally re-living the moment. "The clues to this whole charade were there then. They had only to be interpreted. And frankly, I found the supposition that Melody had actually been impaled by an arrow (and—tch! tch!—through the skull) extremely hard to accept. Not an impossible feat, mind you, just difficult, and highly improbable."

"Then how—?"

"You may recall, Mr. Conklin, that the pillow of the mattress had two holes in it. One, where your sister's head might well have rested, and the other in the material on the underside of the mattress. If the mattress was inflated at the time (and it must have been, to support the weight of our unhappy victim) then those two rupture points would have been several inches apart. When you weigh this observation against that of the arrow having projected a meager inch beyond the back of the skull, the discrepancy becomes untenable. A bullet, I was quick to assume, would more logically have made those holes."

"But the arrow was there," Conklin insisted.

"Yes, it was. But I would think it more likely that the arrow had been inserted into a hole that had first been reamed through by a bullet. And to support this premise, there was the interior matter that appeared to have been pushed out ahead of the arrow. Had the arrow gone through the skull with the speed and force necessary for that kind of penetration, it would have done so (in my opinion) cleanly. It would have tended to sear and cauterize the wound and, ultimately, to prevent such leakage by its very presence."

Conklin raised his eyes to the ceiling in a gesture of utter frustration. "What you're saying now, lieutenant, is that Melody was not killed by the arrow, that she was shot by Slade, but he did not kill her, and that she was already dead before he did it. Will you kindly get to the mother-lovin' point?"

"The point is, Mr. Conklin, that Melody was not killed by an arrow or a bullet. She was asphyxiated. The blue, mottled appearance of her face was the first attestation of that. And, I might add, the unusual absence of any meaningful bleeding would further suggest that her heart had stopped pumping, well before her skull had been punctured, by whatever means."

Conklin straightened excitedly. "But—but, lieutenant. If what you say is true: that Slade didn't kill her, and Crampton only "diverted the course of justice" (as you so aptly put it), and that I am the only innocent one here, then that just leaves—"

"Yes, Mr. Conklin. That leaves—Helen Mundy."

The troubled eyes of Helen Mundy met those of the Amazon for the first time since she had entered the squad room. The paralyzing fear that had gripped her appeared now to have abated, and it seemed almost with a measure of relief that she now faced her accuser. Her voice, when she spoke, was a fragile whisper.

"You've known all along, haven't you?"

"Just about."

"And all along, I've known that you knew. I could sense it. I'm glad now that it's over." Her eyes blinked at the gathering moisture.

"But how could you be so certain, lieutenant, just from the way she looked, the blotches—?"

"There was also the unexplainable abrasion on the side of her neck," the Amazon put in quietly.

"Yes, but that could so easily have been self-inflicted—in so many ways. Surely, you had more to go on than that."

"In the main lounge," the Amazon recalled, "you were eminently more startled by the fact that Melody had been shot, than you were from the news of her death (as was Slade, when he first heard about the arrow). You had left her, dead, from asphyxiation; Slade had left her, dead (or so he supposed), from a gun shot wound. It must have been a disconcerting moment for both of you."

Miss Mundy breathed a low reflective sigh and looked over at Slade. His pasty face was expressionless, his eyes were empty hollows. The maggots seemed to have drawn quietly back into their holes.

"It was not until we searched your rooms, Miss Mundy, and I saw the polyurethane tote bag, that I realized how you had managed it. Until then, drowning had seemed to be the only means at your disposal, but that didn't coincide with the way the body had floated so high in the water, with the air so obviously still trapped in the lungs. The M.E.'s report, by the way, has since confirmed asphyxiation as the mode of death, and conversely, ruled out drowning. But it was the wet leather drawstring that put the clincher on it."

"It was her own damn fault," Helen Mundy sobbed into the crumpled tissue. "She just wouldn't keep her mouth shut."

"It was then, of course, when she threatened to expose you, that you decided to silence her, once and for good. How long could it have taken to empty the tote bag of its contents—one, two seconds—and then to slip it over Melody's unsuspecting head?" The girl's dark hair covered her face and hands as she wept uncontrollably. "Then by expelling the excess air with the flat of your hands, and tightening the leather thong—"

"Oh God." Conklin had cradled his head in his heavy hands. "And we were right there, watching it happen."

"The clear plastic of the bag could hardly be noticed from that distance," the Amazon pointed out, "even had you been looking for it. The drawstring, of course, is what caused the abrasion on her neck, and the inevitable struggle that ensued was the 'splashing about' that you had attributed to the pool therapy."

"But how could she have gotten Melody onto that mattress without our seeing?"

The lieutenant directed the query to the distraught woman. "Miss Mundy?"

"I—I didn't," she replied after a tortured pause. Her hysteria had lapsed into a series of jerking sobs. "I—slid the mattress under her, using the side of the pool as a kind of - of third hand. It's a maneuver I learned in a life-saving class when I—I was a teen."

"And then (correct me if I'm wrong) you loosened the air valve in the mattress so that it would deflate slowly, giving you time to leave and to establish an alibi. Then, when everyone had left the scene, the weight of your victim (who appeared to those on the patio, to be happily sunbathing) would eventually sink into the pool along with the deflated air mattress. You had set the stage, Miss Mundy, for what you hoped would seem to be an accidental drowning. Unfortunately, as in most unpremeditated crimes, you overlooked so many things."

Helen Mundy's pretty face was twisted in anguish and the eyes she lifted to the podium were red-rimmed and glazed with fear.

"Are you prepared now to make a statement, Miss Mundy?"

The girl nodded dispiritedly, and the policewoman, on some obscure signal, moved in quickly. Helen Mundy accepted her escort's hand on her arm without protest until they had reached the door to the hall. Here, she stopped abruptly, and turned.

"The arrow." Her voice was a thin, bewildered plea. "How could the arrow—?"

The lieutenant condoned the delay with a slight lift of her chin. "That was Mr. Crampton's contribution, Miss Mundy. You said yourself you passed him on the road as you left the ranch. Mr. Conklin, having driven south, would logically not have seen him. In any case, he arrived back at the house just in time to witness Melody's 'second demise'. He simply hid, and waited, until he saw Stephen Slade drive away. And it was then that he went about the grisly and appalling task of inserting the arrow into the hole that had been made by Slade's bullet."

Crampton, oblivious to all, licked a dehydrated lip and belched dispassionately. His crapulent expression reflected only the relief that had come with the gastric eruption.

Conklin glared at the grounds man with intense loathing. "But why? For the love of God, why—?"

"By the terms of your late father's will, Mr. Conklin (which I will never live long enough to fully comprehend), this bibulous reprobate had been bequeathed an annual annuity of approximately eight-thousand dollars, until the ripe old age of seventy-five. That is, unless both principal beneficiaries (yourself and Melody) should pre-decease him."

"Yes, I know, but—"

"But, Mr. Conklin, that was the key. If given that unlikely circumstance, the will granted a proviso of commutation which, in layman's terms, was the right to receive the annuity in one lump sum, rather than have it doled out to him in small amounts over the next thirty-six years. Crampton, of course, was delighted by the death of one beneficiary, and he reasoned (if we may be permitted to use the word that loosely) that should you also be eliminated, he would have effectively removed both legal obstacles to his right of commutation, in one fell swoop. The bow and arrow charade was perpetrated in the belief that you would be suspected al principio, as the only person on the ranch capable of killing Melody in that particular manner. He undoubtedly saw you, in his besotted mind's eye, being charged, held for trial and, eventually, executed, in place of the real murderer whom he believed to be Slade. Slade, he knew, could never pose a threat to him without putting his own neck in a noose."

Conklin was staring at Crampton with his mouth open. "Incredible," he breathed.

"What he actually stood to gain, Mr. Conklin, was thirty-six years of eight-thousand per, or, two-hundred and eighty thousand dollars, in one lump sum. Almost enough to buy a small brewery."

As Helen Mundy was led silently away, the other officer moved into the room and tapped Stephen Slade on the shoulder. "Follow me," he said flatly, and turning to Crampton, "you too."

Mark could not repress a smile as he watched them leave, with Crampton bringing up the rear, carroming off both sides of the door as he stumbled through it.

In the meantime, Conklin had risen to his feet. He approached the podium with his western hat gripped knuckle tight in his ham-like hands.

"Lieutenant," he faltered, "I—I'd like to apologize—I didn't realize—"

Lieutenant Carruthers offered her hand to the rancher with a forgiving smile. "It's a big man, Mr. Conklin, who can say he's sorry."

When finally they were alone, the Amazon turned to Mark almost shyly. "I haven't thanked you yet, for the Valentine," she said, warming him with a smile that was worth roughly two years of his pension. "I'm not too sure, though," she added, "whether I'm being hallowed—or hassled."

"Don't you?"

"The Amazon gave her two i.c. a long look. When their eyes met, she said softly, "And then again, I guess I do."

To Mom Without Love

Originally published in *Mike Shane Mystery Magazine*, June 1982.

SHE WAS MURDERED ON MOTHER'S DAY.

They were seated at the long table in the dining room, all eight of them, with mother Julia Endicott at the head. A festive occasion, with flowers, and candelabra, and champagne in long-stemmed glasses. The entire family was there; mother, of course, three sons and a daughter, and three more, kindred by marriage. Karl, the eldest, had risen to his feet, and was in the process of offering up a toast "on this propitious day," to all the mothers of the world, and his own in particular, when a muffled explosion echoed like distant thunder down the length of the table. Seven pairs of eyes turned as one to see mother Endicott's gentle face flare in sudden, exquisite agony. And as they sat rooted to their chairs, the tortured features turned grimly pale, then slowly, silently slumped, as in an old silent movie, to descend squarely into her plate of roast prime rib and Yorkshire pudding, with a dull unpalatable plop.

No one moved. Karl remained on his feet in stunned immobility. It was Elsa, Karl's wife, who finally pushed back her chair and went to the woman's side. "She's dead," she said after a close examination. "She's been shot. Someone had better call the police."

* * * *

Detective-Lieutenant Cathy Carruthers stood at her office window in Metro Central's Eleventh Precinct, a superb silhouette against the blood red sky of a dying day. Beyond the window, lights were winking on in the deepening crimson dusk and slow-moving streams of traffic had already begun the ritual daily blood-letting from the city's heart. She looked to be deep in thought.

"A penny for your dreams, lieutenant."

She started, then turned with a wry smile as Detective-Sergeant Mark Swanson's imposing frame filled the open doorway.

"Wouldn't thoughts be more precise?"

Mark shrugged his heavy shoulders. "Who wants precise?" he said. "I live and breathe precise." His ruggedly handsome features took on a distant look. "It's dreams, lieutenant, that can turn a man into a lion—a woman into a tigress." He growled softly.

The lieutenant chuckled as she took the chair behind her desk. "Enough already," she protested. "Lions and tigers make lousy detectives. So do dreamers." She tilted her beautiful blonde head. "What's on the agenda?"

Mark dumped his hefty carcass into a chair with a disparaging grunt, leveling a wistful eye at his senior partner. Six magnificent feet of honey-haired female could be a monumental distraction at the best of times, but working two i.c. to the "Amazon," as she was known to her burly colleagues in Homicide, had been a bucket of mixed blessings for Mark, and an exercise in manly frustrations. His good-natured verbal passes (and her mild rebukes) had lately become routine. A thinly veiled attempt, perhaps, to self-censor the deep bond of respect and mutual affection that had grown between them.

"There's been a killing," Mark began, "out in Thornston Heights. You know the area, Mortgage Hill, where Metro's "elite" live. A guy by the name of Karl DeVries phoned it in. He claims someone shot his mother."

The lieutenant arched a flawless eyebrow. " His mother? Mark, isn't this Mother's Day?"

"Right on lieutenant. Sunday, May 9th."

"Tch, tch—Well, so much for mother-love." She hooked an unruly lock of spun gold from her forehead with an elegantly curled middle-finger. "Suspects?"

"Seven. All family. They were having dinner at the time."

"Then we know who did it?"

Mark shook his head as he raked a wooden match across the sole of his shoe and touched the flame to a cigarette. "No one saw a thing."

"Nothing?"

"Nothing."

"Hmm." The lieutenant seemed to see something of interest on the ceiling. "That's a bit unusual. Still, matricides of this type are not normally too complicated. The silent seven will probably turn out to be one murderer and six reluctant witnesses. Everything being equal, Mark, I'd guess a quick wrap-up on this one."

Mark drew heavily on the cigarette. "You can forget the everything-being-equal, lieutenant. This guy DeVries is a psychiatrist, his wife is his nurse. He said they made a cursory check of the victim before he phoned. She'd been shot all right, but the only wound they could find was in the abdomen."

"So?"

"It was an exit wound."

"So? again."

"There was no entry wound."

"That's not possible, Mark. What came out must have gone in. Somewhere."

"Yeah, well—it's got DeVries flipping through his own inkblots."

The lieutenant placed the tips of her fingers and thumbs together, pressed them to her lips and closed her eyes. She almost looked to be praying. Mark knew better. Preying, he thought, might be more to the point. "Mark," she said at last, "unless bullets have started to make U turns, we might just have a puzzler on our hands."

Mark gave her a knowing grin. The Amazon, he knew, was in her element. There was nothing that intrigued her more than a "puzzler."

"I've already alerted the meat squad," Mark said, pushing himself out of the chair. "They'll be there ahead of us. And there was a black-n-white in the neighborhood, lieutenant. Fisk and Mayhew. I gave them instructions to get individual statements from the seven suspects, and to keep them on the premises, under escort. They're all related, one way or another, to the victim, Julia Endicott."

"Endicott? I thought you said the man's name was DeVries."

"I did, and it is. DeVries is apparently Julia Endicott's son from a former marriage. And apart from his wife, Elsa, each of the other six is either an Endicott, or married to one. Same mother, different father."

"I see." The lieutenant humored him with a doubtful smile. "We'll sort that out later." She rose from the chair, smoothed the creases from her snug gray skirt, slipped a matching jacket over a form-fitting white shirt-blouse (much to Mark's disappointment) and shouldered a well-worn red leather purse.

"Let's go," she said, as she made for the door. "Let's find out just what kind of person would actually kill their own mother—on Mother's Day."

The Endicott home typified the old-world affluence of Thornston Heights. It was an ancient rambling colonial on half an acre of extravagant landscaping. Lawns were vast and green, flower beds rife with color, and a mingling of stately pines and poplars embraced the brooding old house with a somber, verdant dignity. A rank of white pillars stood guard at the entrance and dark-lidded dormers, like armed loopholes, seemed to defend a way of life that was already history. There were a dozen vehicles in the parking lot, six of them police cars, when Mark and Lieutenant Carruthers pulled up in an unmarked Chevy.

"We're not exactly the early birds, are we?"

Mark with a sly grin, was quick to point out that birds did not make any better detectives than lions and tigers. The lieutenant winced. "Touche," she said. And a moment later, she had slipped out of the car and was headed off across the gravel toward the house. Mark caught up quickly, coasting into step beside her.

They climbed wide stone steps to a kind of portico, where a black uniformed officer, the size of Too Tall Jones, stood stoically before the door. He directed them across a large entrance hall, through a lavishly furnished lounge, and into a dining room that still smelled pleasantly of food. The candelabra continued to burn brightly over the table but what was left of the champagne had all but given up its last bubble. The tragic figure of Julia Endicott was still firmly ensconced in her half-eaten dinner.

Sam Morton, Chief Medical Examiner for Metro Central, looked up from the body as they entered.

"Ah, lieutenant. Glad you're here. I've been waiting to get this lady onto a stretcher."

"Have the camera crew done their thing, Sam?"

"Just finished."

The lieutenant's vivid blue eyes turned grimly cold as she methodically surveyed the scene of the crime. Were it not for the missing dinner guests, the shooting could have taken place just a moment before. Chairs were pushed back from the table, as though in a kind of panic, and uneaten portions of roast beef and pudding had been left to cool on the plates. Someone, the lieutenant noted, had already chalked the outline of the body and its relative position to the table, the chair, and the floor.

"Okay," she said, "but do it carefully. I don't want anything disturbed. And Sam, I'd like a preliminary as soon as possible."

"No problem, lieutenant. I can give it to you now, but I don't think you're going to like it."

"Oh?"

"Well, for starters, she's been shot."

"That's very astute, Sam."

Sam Morgan grinned good-naturedly. "This lady's been shot, lieutenant, from the inside—out."

"Can you be more explicit?"

"The body has only one wound that I can see. It's in the abdomen. And it's an exit wound."

"Come on, Sam. If a bullet did an exit through her stomach, it must have entered somewhere."

"Tell me more, lieutenant."

The Amazon acknowledged his sarcasm with a lopsided smile. "What about the body's natural orifices?"

"Not likely."

"But you're not certain."

"That's right, lieutenant, I'm not. This is a prelim, remember? The "I'm certains" will have to wait until after the autopsy."

"Was there more than one bullet?"

"I doubt it."

"Has anyone found the one there was?"

"Not to my knowledge."

"Anything else you can tell me, Sam?"

"Not really—except, judging from the hole it made coming out, I wouldn't think there'd be much of a bullet left to find."

"That's encouraging."

With the aid of an assistant, Sam Morton moved the lifeless mother Endicott from her seat of honor at the table to a waiting stretcher. They were about to wheel it away when the lieutenant leaned over the body, peering closely at the grisly wound.

"Just a moment, Sam. What are these little black flecks in the wound?"

"You're guess is as good as mine, lieutenant. Maybe she put too much pepper on her roast beef. Jeeeez, let me do my job, will you? I'll write a whole book about it, later. Much later. Yeah—I'll call it the Autopsy Report, by Samuel Morgan, M.D., and I'll personally see to it that you get a free autographed copy sometime tomorrow. Now will you please let me get the hell outta here?"

The lieutenant watched him go with a wide grin. She turned to Mark who had stooped to inspect the wood behind the blood-splattered table cloth.

"Find anything?"

Mark opened a pen knife and dug gingerly at the polished wood. "Just a few lead fragments, lieutenant. Very soft lead. Scattered. Hardly penetrated the varnish." He dropped his gaze and his hands to the carpet beneath the table's edge, combing the thick pile with his fingers. "There's a few fragments down here, too."

"The lieutenant examined a piece of the soft metal. "I want this whole table area gone over thoroughly by the Lab team," she said to Mark, "with particular attention given to the underside of the table. Regardless of how it was done, we must assume that this woman was shot. And whoever shot her was apparently sitting at this table. Since no one saw it happen, we can only conclude that the gun was fired from below the table, out of sight of the others."

"Gotcha." Mark was quick to pick up her train of thought. "A paraffin scan under the table would not only tell us if a gun was fired, but where it was fired from. All we'd have to do then, would be to find who was sitting where at the table. And if the suspects were tested as well, a positive match-up on one of them would give us a pretty tight case. Maybe you were right, lieutenant, about a quick wrap-up, I mean."

"We should be so lucky."

Mark's enthusiasm quickly ebbed. "You don't think we'd have a case?"

"It's all too easy, Mark." The lieutenant was slowly circling the long table. "Too pat, somehow. Besides, we still don't know how that bullet (or whatever it was), managed to come bursting out of the lady's stomach when it had no obvious way of getting in."

"Any ideas?"

"Well—one possible solution might be a bullet that had been rigged to explode on impact. The explosion at the skin's surface could conceivably give the illusion of an exit wound, even if, in fact, it was not."

"Yeah." Mark brightened. "It might at that. But will Sam be able to pick that up in the autopsy?"

"I don't see why not."

"Then we'll just have to wait for the autopsy report." Mark grinned, remembering Sam's parting edict. "—sometime tomorrow."

"Not necessarily, Mark." The lieutenant was standing behind the chair at the foot of the table, looking down its cluttered length. "If an impact slug was used, and only one shot was fired, there would have to be (not one, but) two reports. One, when the bullet left the gun, the other, when it exploded on impact. And the other six witnesses—"

"Of course." Mark thumped his head with the heel of his hand. "Lieutenant, you never cease to amaze me. Mind you, DeVries never mentioned hearing two reports, but then he didn't mention hearing only one, either. Maybe it's time we started asking a few questions."

The lieutenant turned as the friendly black giant entered the room with a precautionary duck of his head. The Lab crew came trailing in behind him.

"Officer, where'd you stash the seven suspects?"

"In the library, lieutenant. The door at the end of the front hall." He pointed behind him. "Officers Fisk and Mayhew are in there now, taking statements."

"Thank you." The lieutenant returned the officer's easy smile with one of her own, then watched him duck out of the room and head back to his post at the front entrance.

"He's a tall one," she said to Mark. "What's his name?"

"Bones."

"As in Jones?"

"Uh-hu. George Washington Bones."

"What do they call him?"

"Too Tall."

The lieutenant looked heavenward as though in search of help. "I'm sorry I asked."

One of the men from the Lab team detached himself from the group. "Anything special on this one, lieutenant?"

"Mark, here, will clue you in, officer. And, Mark, you might have them drop off a sample of that lead you found, to Ballistics. I've never known a slug fragment to be so pliable. When you're through, I'll be in the library."

"You got it, lieutenant."

As she turned to go, all eyes went with her, like a well-trained drill team. They followed her engaging back through the dining room door and across the vast carpeted floor of the lounge, metering her long-legged loping stride with awe and approbation. When she reached the door to the hall, those same eyes suddenly jerked wide in shock.

"Stop him!"

The frantic shout had come from the direction of the library. Too late. A man came hurtling through the doorway like a bull out of loading chute. Taken by surprise, the lieutenant was dumped roughly to one side, momentarily staggered. The intruder had run clear into the center of the lounge before he spotted Mark and the Lab team. He was cut off. He had obviously tried to detour around Too Tall Bones, whose massive frame was literally obliterating the front entrance. But now, with escape thwarted a second time, he swung quickly around and headed back the way he had come. A flushed and shaken Cathy Carruthers apparently did not strike him as being much of a threat.

That was his mistake.

This time, the Amazon saw him coming. In one unbroken, fluid movement, she hiked up her snug gray skirt, well past the midway mark of her long thighs, and swung to face him (which in itself, Mark thought later, should have been enough to stop any man) and with the reptilian grace of a striking cobra, she drove a nylon-clad knee fiercely into the man's stomach. He collapsed in pain and nausea. But before he could hit the floor, the Amazon had spun around, her golden mane flying, and with one hand at his collar, the other at the seat of his pants, she blithely picked him up and started down the hall with him, toward the library. The man's feet were churning thin air a good foot above the floor.

"I don't believe it," said one of the Lab men.

"I don't believe them," said another.

"Hey, Swanson," a third man said to Mark, "where do you get the brownie points to play in the same sandbox with that carnivorous kitten?"

Mark eyed the man grimly. "First off," he said, in a soft menacing voice, "you gotta be able to shift a motor-mouth outta high gear, and into neutral."

The Lab men went quietly to work on the table.

When Mark caught up with the lieutenant, she was standing in front of a red tile fireplace in the library, with policewoman Fisk at one elbow, and officer Mayhew at the other. They spoke in low voices, comparing notes, while the other seven people in the room sat quietly waiting. Book shelves lined all four walls with only a high narrow window here and there, and the door, to break the continuum of hoarded knowledge. An occasional moan drifted up from a deep leather chair where the would-be escapee was slouched low, nursing his stomach.

"You, then, are James Endicott," the lieutenant said to the moan. When it failed to answer, officer Fisk said, "That's him, lieutenant. He answers to Jimmy—at times."

"What made him bolt out of here?"

The officer shrugged her shoulders. "He just didn't like being detained, I guess. He said he had a heavy date. He's the youngest of three sons, lieutenant. Twenty-six. Not married. And not terribly broken up, it seems, at the death of his mother."

"Occupation?"

"He's a gentleman of, uh—leisure." Officer Fisk's soft brown eyes looked almost apologetic. "He told me he 'subsists' on an allowance from his father's estate. He would not divulge the amount."

The lieutenant looked at the young man in question with mild disfavor. "Gentleman, you say."

"Lieutenant?"

An untidy looking man who appeared to be in his early forties, stood up as he spoke. He was dressed in a tweed jacket, with leather elbows, and a badly trimmed full beard. A curved pipe drooped congenitally from a protruding lower lip. There was a patronizing manner about him that he was given to flaunt like a badge of merit. This man, Mark guessed, bearing all the usual sad pretensions of the academic milieu, would no doubt be the psychiatrist.

"I'm Karl DeVries," the man unwittingly confirmed. "This is my wife, Elsa."

The woman who had now risen to his side, was forbiddingly austere in a shapeless black dress. Her hair was straight, without fullness or color, and her thin sharp face gave her the look of a gaunt wingless bird.

"Do we not have your statement?" the lieutenant asked the psychiatrist.

"Yes, you do. Officer Mayhew took it, but—"

"But, what?"

"Well, Elsa and I examined the wound, lieutenant, before I made the phone call, and there just isn't any way it could have happened—"

"But it did happen," the lieutenant said curtly.

"Yes, well—perhaps you could tell me if you've found out how or who—I mean, there was only one—"

The lieutenant bristled. "I do not intend to discuss the complicacies of this case with you, sir, nor the progress of our investigation. You are a suspect, Mr. DeVries, nothing more. Now please sit down."

"Doctor," DeVries said, obviously miffed at being so abruptly dismissed.

"Eh?"

"Doctor DeVries," the man insisted.

The lieutenant regarded him coolly, then left him with an irreverent "Hmph" as she turned her attention back to officer Fisk's notebook. "Now, which of you is Julia Endicott's daughter?" she asked the room at large.

A woman about thirty, with long flowing auburn hair and a pleasant round face, raised her hand. "I am, lieutenant. I'm Susan Endicott—I mean, Cross." She giggled nervously at her own confusion. "I've been an Endicott for thirty years, and a Cross for one. I guess I'm just not used to it yet." She looked sheepishly at the man beside her. "This is my husband, Brian."

Brian Cross had an affable, easy way about him. He was younger than his wife, deeply tanned, with boyish good looks and a shock of blonde hair that had been bleached almost white by the sun. He returned her embarrassed look with an understanding smile and reached for her hand.

"What's your occupation, Mr. Cross?"

"I'm, uh—between jobs, lieutenant."

"What did you do previously?"

"He's a competitor," Mrs. Cross put in quickly, defensively. "He's a top ranking surfer. We've just come back from Hawaii where he placed—"

"Top ranking beach bum, you mean."

The unfriendly interruption had come from a man who could only be Herman J. Endicott (being the only unidentified man left) and, according to officer Mayhew's notes, a bank manager by profession. The woman at his side, the lieutenant assumed, would be his wife, Cybil.

"What bank are you with, Mr. Endicott?"

"Metro Civic Savings," the man replied.

Herman J. Endicott not only was a banker, he looked like one. He had a huge pudgy body that was (at the moment, at least) humanely hidden from view beneath the folds of an expensive gray business suit, but three obscenely bloated chins still remained, unadorned, in the public domain. Sitting there, with his lard and his chins, and a pair of thick-rimmed spectacles perched on a dab-of-putty nose, he looked for all the world like a giant pink frog in mufti. His wife, Cybil, who obviously shared his table as well as his lily pad, was only sightly less obese than he.

"Ribbit, ribbit—"

The humiliating sound had come from somewhere in the vicinity of an angelic looking Brian Cross. Herman J. glowered at his handsome young brother-in-law who, in turn, politely acknowledged the glower with a nod and a smile. Susan Cross dug an elbow into her husband's ribs, then seemed to find something amusing in her lap.

"Please?"

Lieutenant Cathy Carruthers waited patiently until the room was silent. All eyes were on her. There were times, Mark mused, when his stunning partner truly put live meat on the bare bones of a mythical jungle legend. The Amazon. A goddess from another planet, he thought, could not have been more incredibly unique, more outrageously beautiful. She stood now with her feet braced firmly apart, hands on hips, chest high, her luminous blue eyes sweeping the room like an airport beacon.

"There are some questions," she told the gathering, "that I'd like to ask you all in unison. Please think carefully before you attempt to answer." She looked to each waiting upturned face before she went on. "Now, was there anyone else, anyone, other than you seven, in or around the house at the time of Mrs. Endicott's death?"

The seven suspects shook their heads as if wired by a single string.

"Not a maid? A handyman? A housekeeper?"

"Not today, lieutenant," Susan Cross volunteered. "There is a full-time housekeeper, a Mrs. Griffith, but she was given the time off while the family was visiting. I helped my mother prepare and serve the dinner." She lowered her eyes, visibly saddened. "She wanted this to be a close family re-union."

"Then you all planned to spend the night?"

"Everyone," Herman J. put in, "but my wife and me. We live only a few blocks away, lieutenant. Besides, we felt it would be crowding things a bit."

"Plenty of room," Jimmy muttered, having suddenly found his voice. "Couple of stuffed shirts, that's all."

The lieutenant ignored the interruption. "Did anyone of you see any kind of weapon—a gun, perhaps?"

The heads moved negatively for a second time.

"Does anyone own a gun?"

"Karl does," Jimmy piped in. "He's a real gun freak. He even makes his own bullets."

The lieutenant turned to face the psychiatrist. "Is that true?"

"I certainly don't consider myself to be a freak, lieutenant, but, yes, I do have an interest in guns."

"You make your own ammunition?"

"Yes. But what I choose to make myself, anyone over eighteen can purchase at will. I fail to see anything sinister, lieutenant, in what has lately become a rather popular hobby."

"Murder," the lieutenant noted quietly, "has also become rather popular of late." She swung her attention back to the group. "The shot," she asked them, "was it loud? Or faint? Muted? What did it sound like?"

"Faint," said Jimmy.

"Muted," said Herman J.

"Muffled," said Susan Cross. She looked at her husband for corroboration.

"Muffled," he agreed with an affable nod.

"Now think, before you answer this last question." The lieutenant paused significantly. "Can any of you remember, precisely, how many shots were fired?"

"One," they answered in a chorus.

The lieutenant's eyes flicked from one face to another. "You're sure of that?"

Jimmy Endicott put voice to their collective response. "One shot," he said unequivocally. The rest of them nodded.

"There goes our solid case," Mark muttered close against Lieutenant Carruthers' ear.

"So it would seem," she sighed. To the seven witnesses, she said, "That's all the questions for now, but I must ask that no one leave this house unless authorized." She disregarded Herman J.'s angry snort. "Guards will be posted to ensure that you comply. I must also ask that you cooperate with officers Fisk and Mayhew while they conduct an immediate search; first, of your persons, then this room, the dining room, the lounge and the kitchen, and the traveled areas between."

The lieutenant spoke to Susan Cross. "Will you be able to accommodate your brother and his wife, Mrs. Cross?"

"Why, of course," she said. "This place has more bedrooms than the Metro Hilton."

"The rates aren't bad either," her husband quipped.

The lieutenant smiled. You could not help but like this pair. To Mark, she said, "I guess it's back to square one for us."

"Yeah." Mark tagged along as she made for the door. "Got any more bright ideas?"

"Just one." She treated him to a win-some-lose-some look. "Let's grab a salami on rye. Maybe we'll 'detect' better on a full stomach."

When the lieutenant and Mark returned to the house on Thornston Hill, an hour and some twenty minutes later, they were met at the door by Too Tall Bones.

"Evening, lieutenant. Sergeant."

Nodding, the lieutenant hesitated. "Have you been relieved for a lunch break, officer?"

"No sweat, lieutenant," the big man replied. He pointed to a brown paper sack just inside the door, big enough to hold a week's groceries. "My wife fixed me a lunch."

"Well, you'd better get at it," the lieutenant said, with a wondering look at the bag. "You're only on shift for another four hours."

Once inside, they found the overnight guests wandering freely about the house. Officers Fisk and Mayhew were seated before the fireplace in the lounge, with their lunch pails open. As the lieutenant and Mark approached, Mayhew was trying to talk the brown-eyed Fisk into swapping a turkey sandwich for one with jelly and peanut butter.

"Forget it, Mayhew," Fisk was saying, "you must think I'm stupid, or something. I didn't burn my brains with my bra, you know—" Her words trailed off into an embarrassed silence as she realized they were no longer alone.

The lieutenant grinned. "Sorry to interrupt such an enlightened discussion, officers, but can I safely assume that you have completed the search I ordered?"

"All done, lieutenant." Mayhew spoke with difficulty around a mouthful of jelly and peanut butter.

Did you turn up a weapon of any kind?"

"No gun, no weapon of any kind—no nothing."

"Hmm—the further we get into this case, the more perplexing it seems to get. Just one dead-end after another." The lieutenant chewed thoughtfully at her lower lip. "Well, let's try extending the search to their homes. We might just turn up a new lead."

"Tonight?" Officer Fisk looked dismayed. "There's three of them out there, lieutenant, not counting Jimmy's quarters, upstairs."

"Two," Mayhew put in. "DeVries lives across the state line in Huntsville. Out of our jurisdiction."

"So now what do we do?" Fisk gulped the last of her turkey sandwich and washed it down with a tug at her thermos.

"You start by checking out young Endicott's rooms, upstairs, then pick up the other two. Herman J. and his wife live only a few blocks from here. The Cross's, if I remember correctly, are out in Beachville, close to the surfing.

"Whatta we do for search warrants?" Mayhew asked.

"You don't." The lieutenant was looking a little exasperated. "You solicit their cooperation. And don't forget their keys."

"What if they refuse?"

"Just remind them that we can always do it the hard way—tomorrow morning. Why delay the inevitable?"

"And DeVries, lieutenant. What about him?"

"Mark will handle it." She turned to her two i.c. "Get on the blower to Huntsville, Mark, and arrange a proxy search of the DeVries home. They'll need time to pick up a warrant, so you better get with it. And don't forget to fill them in on the case so they'll know what to look for."

"What are we looking for?" Fisk asked ingenuously.

The lieutenant regarded the young brunette with measured patience. "We're looking for three of those five illusive Ws, officer Fisk. We already have the When and the Where. It's the What, Why and Who we're after now. Are there any more stupid questions?"

No one seemed inclined to risk her further displeasure by responding. It wasn't until the lieutenant and Mark were half way across the room that officer Fisk found the courage to call after them. "Lieutenant?"

The big blonde detective halted abruptly and slowly turned, then stood, silent, watching the young policewomen apprehensively narrow the gap between them.

"I don't know if this is important," the officer said meekly, "but I found it in the kitchen during our search." She held out a blue plastic folder about the size of a large wallet, loosely wrapped in a paper napkin. It had a white label affixed to the front of it. "It's a prescription, lieutenant. The label is made out to Julia Endicott."

The lieutenant took the folder and read the label aloud. "Three capsules a day, before meals." She opened it. Both interior sides were lined with a series of small celluloid pockets, each about a half inch in diameter, and most of which still contained a deep red gelatin capsule.

"Very good, officer Fisk." The lieutenant rewarded the young rookie with a smile. "This could prove helpful."

Officer Fisk beamed.

Following his call to Huntsville, Mark went in search of his senior partner. He found her in the library, seated at a small reading table. She had the plastic prescription folder before her, studying it closely. She looked up as he entered.

"Mark, have a look at this."

He drew a chair up beside her as she edged the folder and herself closer to him. He was not unhappy with the resulting shoulder-rubbing propinquity.

"You can see, Mark, how the prescribed capsules are arranged chronologically on each side of the folder. Three in each row (breakfast, lunch and dinner), seven rows on each side; in all, a two-week supply. And see how each row of three is dated." She pointed with a brightly lacquered, blood-red fingertip. "She apparently began taking them at breakfast on May 4th, here, which is the first date shown. Now, notice that all the celluloid pockets on this left side, are empty (May 4th through May 9th), except for the last row, dated May 10th. That means she took her medication, whatever it was, up to, and including, the one before her fateful last dinner."

Mark's face reflected the puzzling turn of his thoughts. "This is all very interesting, lieutenant, but aren't we dealing with a shooting?"

"Indeed we are, Mark. But what if one of these capsules had contained an explosive of some kind?"

"Come again, lieutenant. There just isn't any way that an explosive charge in a casing that small, could carry a detonating timer—or even some far-out kind of remote electrical impulse mechanism. It just is not physically possible."

"It isn't physically possible for a bee to fly, Mark, but it damn well does."

"Meaning?"

"Impossible, is not one of my favorite words."

"I'll remember that," Mark confided meaningfully, "next time I get a couple of tickets to the ball park."

The slow unfolding of her wide grin at such close quarters, Mark decided, was tantamount to watching the parting of the Red Sea.

"Am I interrupting anything, lieutenant?"

The two detectives drew apart like a couple of errant kids. Susan Cross stood in the doorway and there was a teasing, knowing twinkle in her eyes.

"No—of course not." This was the first time Mark had ever seen Cathy Carruthers in less than total control of her composure. "What can I do for you?"

"I'd like your permission to clean up the dining room, lieutenant. Brian and Jimmy have offered to help."

"Yes, well—" The lieutenant straightened authoritatively with a defiant toss of her honey-colored tresses. "I see no reason why you can't. As a matter of fact, I plan to use that room, hopefully sometime tomorrow, for a revelatory reenactment of the crime."

"We'll have it ready for you, lieutenant." She turned and quickly left.

"Where were we?" Mark asked innocently.

"Where we've been since we took on this case," the lieutenant replied in a brisk, back-to-business voice, "back at square one—where else?"

It was the following day, Monday, May 10th. Cathy Carruthers sat nursing a cup of coffee at a table in Lil Oly's Cafeteria, one short block from the Eleventh Precinct. Her attention seemed to vacillate between the papers she had spread out over the table, and the entrance to the cafeteria, The noon lunch crowd had thinned to a few stragglers and she was beginning to show signs of mild exacerbation when Mark's husky frame suddenly filled the doorway. Her eyes brightened as she returned his friendly glance of recognition.

She watched with amusement as he headed directly for the coffee bar, while dogging tenaciously in his footsteps, a little man, taking three steps to Mark's one, followed close behind. She recognized at once the abbreviated Garfield Leprohn, Metro Central's shortest police officer, and the controversial head of the Records Department. Mark seemed to be totally unmindful of the little guy who struggled along in his wake, trying desperately to keep up, while balancing a cup of coffee in one hand and a briefcase in the other. When finally they were seated at the lieutenant's table, the Leprechaun, as he was known to his life-sized colleagues at the precinct, sank back in his chair and breathed an audible sigh of relief.

"Whew!" he gasped. "I'm a little short on breath." He glanced at Mark, regretting at once his unhappy choice of words.

"What else is new?" Mark muttered dryly. He seemed incapable of resisting any opportunity to rub the little cop the wrong way.

The lieutenant fought back a smile as she gathered up the scattered papers and fed them into two separate file folders. She then leveled her startling blue eyes at the Leprechaun.

"Thank you for coming, Garfield. What have you got for me?"

The lieutenant's courtesy in calling him by his given name, instead of that ugly Irish epithet, was not lost on the Records man. "I've got a run-down on all the suspects, including DeVries," he said brightly, basking in the warmth of the lieutenant's smile. "Would you like a summary?"

"Please."

Mark bristled while the little man made a Hollywood production out of opening his briefcase and extracting, one by irritating one, a number of manilla folders from its hidden recesses. Finally, Mark raised one curled fist in front of his eyes and rotated the other as though he was turning an old-fashioned movie camera. "Mummy's Little Helper Tells All," he announced in the servile tones of a Hollywood set director, "take one."

The Leprechaun flushed angrily. "All these people," he began between clenched teeth, "are without a police record of any kind. The Herman J. Endicotts are an integral part of Metro's exclusive upper crust. Socialites, of the first order. On the other hand, young Jimmy Endicott, and the Cross's, are only tolerated. The DeVries, as you know, reside in Huntsville, where they keep pretty much to themselves."

The Leprechaun paused to take a sip of coffee. "Jimmy Endicott, in spite of his immaturity, is warmly embraced by his peers, and grudgingly respected by his elders. He was the favorite son, in every sense of the word."

"That doesn't seem to jibe with the uncaring way he reacted to his mother's death," Mark observed.

"That business back at the house, Mark, was most likely just a gut reaction," the lieutenant replied. "Each one of us has to deal with grief in our own way."

"Yes, well—if Jimmy was the favorite son, then Susan was the favorite (if, only) daughter." The Leprechaun plowed relentlessly on. "And Brian Cross, her husband—well, he's just an out-and-out enigma. He graduated with honors in corporate law, but subsequently rejected numerous, lucrative offers to stand before the bar. He did a voluntary stint in Nam, then gravitated to a wastrel's life with the sun-sand-and-sea set of southern California. About thirteen months ago, he met and married Susan Endicott. In short, this obviously talented young man, aided and abetted now by a coddled wife, has simply turned his back on success to become a beach bum."

"Hmm," the lieutenant mused. "Perhaps one should stop to ponder the true definition of success, Garfield."

The Leprechaun chose not to respond. "DeVries is currently registered at Huntsville U.," he continued. "He's been there most of his adult life; first as a student, then as tenured faculty. He now enjoys his own practice while still affiliated with the university on an honorary basis. Quite a lucrative arrangement. And prior to their marriage, (some six years ago), his wife worked with a pharmaceutical firm. She is now his nurse and receptionist. The DeVries, by the way, are not much liked, apparently—by anyone."

Mark took out a cigarette and lit it. "All this seems to bear out the results (or lack of them) of the searches made by Fisk and Mayhew last night," he said. "They didn't turn up a damn thing, either. Mind you, we still don't have anything yet on the Huntsville call." He squinted thoughtfully at the Leprechaun. "What about the money angle?"

"The banker," replied the Leprechaun, referring to his endless heap of data, "is wealthy in his own right. The rest of them depend, with varying degrees, on Endicott money, voluntarily meted out by mother Endicott. I say 'Endicott money' but it is (or was) DeVries money. Julia Endicott was a wealthy widow with one small son, Karl, when she met and married Walter J. Endicott. Endicott died of prostatic cancer about a year and a half ago, but Julia had never relinquished control of her first husband's money—until, of course, yesterday. There is a will, which was only recently drawn up, leaving the entire estate to all her children equally—"

"There goes the money motive," Mark put in.

"—but it was never signed."

"Oh? Why not?"

"Well, that's what this Mother's Day dinner was all about. She was going to sign it in front of everyone."

"Interesting," the lieutenant reflected, "but not very helpful. The more info we get, the less we seem to know."

"No hidden debts?" Mark probed hopefully.

"None that I could dig up."

Mark turned to his senior partner. "What about Lab, lieutenant, and Ballistics?"

"Another blank. The capsules contained a common medication for chronic osteoarthritis. There were no powder burns (or residues) under, over, or anywhere near the table, except, of course, directly in front of where Mrs. Endicott was sitting. All paraffin tests were negative. Can you believe it? No one at the table fired a gun."

Mark blew a billowing cloud of smoke (with malice aforethought) directly toward the Leprechaun. "Maybe Sam Morton was right," Mark recalled. "Remember what he said, This lady's been shot, lieutenant, from the inside—out."

The lieutenant gathered up her folders. "Yes, and anybody who makes a statement like that had better come up with some answers to back it up." She got to her feet, "Let's go find out what they are."

Before vacating his chair, Mark unleashed another billow of smoke at the Leprechaun. The little man coughed and reached for a cigarette of his own.

"Do you think that's wise?" Mark asked.

"Wise?"

"Cigarettes," Mark grinned, as he turned to leave, "have been known to stunt your growth."

It was after three o'clock when Mark swung the unmarked Chevy out of the Metro Morgue parking lot. The lieutenant sat beside him, clutching her collection of folders in one hand while bracing herself against the dashboard with the other. "Now I know why they call this the suicide seat," she complained, as Mark made a taxi stop at the curb, then hung a ferris-wheel right out onto the main drag.

"Keep your shirt on, lieutenant. We're not in orbit yet."

"Mark," the lieutenant's voice was menacingly quiet. "I have no more intention of going into orbit with you than I have of removing my shirt. Now, slow this vehicle down to legal speed."

Mark decided it would be expedient to change the subject with the gears. "So what's the M.E. got to say?"

With a parting glance at the speedometer, the lieutenant opened one of the files. "Hmm, what's this?"

"Looks like a will," Mark proffered with a quick sidelong glance.

"It is a will," the lieutenant said as she leafed through the legal document, "and it is still unsigned. Now how in blazes did the Leprechaun know that, when it must have gone with the dead woman to the morgue?"

"You just can't sell that little guy short," Mark acknowledged with a wide grin.

The lieutenant muttered something under her breath as she consulted the autopsy report. "Here's what was found in her stomach," she said after a short perusal, "or what was left of it: one empty shell casing, .22 caliber, short—inch-long length of twisted wire (from the roast beef, do you suppose?)—globules of partially dissolved gelatin—minute lead fragments—wide-spread cauterizing of tissue—powder residues—"

Mark emitted a low whistle. "That lady sure had a belly full."

Just what you might expect, Mark, if you can buy a bullet being fired from inside someone's stomach. Oh, here's something else: detonation in mid to lower sector of stomach—rupture of anterior and posterior wall—shell casing reversing through pancreas—lodged solidly against first lumbar vertebrae—" The lieutenant looked quizzically at her two i.c. "What do you make of it, Mark?"

"Not a damn thing. You?"

"Well, for one thing, it proves, unequivocally, a bullet was fired from inside Julia Endicott's stomach."

"Uh-hu." Mark voiced his disbelief. "You said so yourself, lieutenant—that just isn't possible."

"Precisely." The Amazon settled back with a smug, satisfied smile. "You see, Mark, when the 'impossible' becomes a fait accompli, the if is no longer in question—only the how."

Mark gave his beautiful partner a searching stare. "Know something, lieutenant? You're weird."

Once again, eight invited guests sat around the long table in the Endicott dining room. On this somber occasion, however, the candelabra had not been lit and there was no champagne in longstemmed glasses. Detective-Lieutenant Cathy Carruthers now occupied the seat at the head of the table where mother Endicott had so abruptly, and so mysteriously met her death less than twenty-four hours before.

In the background, Mark was making himself as inconspicuous as possible. Officer Fisk stood at the entrance to the kitchen, while Too Tall Bones hovered like a dark cloud just outside the open door to the lounge. Officer Mayhew had assumed the post at the front entrance. The time was precisely 5:35 P.M.

The lieutenant surveyed the seven anxious faces that ringed the table with a cool candor. "You are all seated just as you were, last evening?"

There were seven assenting nods.

Elsa DeVries sat to the lieutenant's left, with Susan Cross next, and then her husband, Brian. On the lieutenant's right was Karl DeVries, Herman J., and his wife, Cybil, in that order. Jimmy Endicott sat alone at the foot of the table. The mood of the group was one of suspense.

"The purpose of this get-together," the lieutenant began, "is to ascertain precisely what happened last evening when Mrs. Julia Endicott—"

"Lieutenant?"

The lieutenant looked up with some annoyance.

"Sorry to interrupt, lieutenant." Too Tall Bones had thrust his great head through the doorway. "Phone call, from Huntsville. They say it's important."

"Thank you, officer." Rising, she said, "Excuse me," to those at the table, then left to take the call.

It was fully five minutes before she returned. All eyes were on her as she resumed her seat.

"A slight change in plans," she announced soberly. "A search of the DeVries' Huntsville home has now given us sufficient substantive evidence to make an arrest. Pardon me, a joint arrest." She turned to the bearded professor on her right. "Suppose you save us all a lot of time and speculation, Mr. DeVries, by telling us just how you armed that deadly capsule that took the life of your mother."

A look of horror clouded the face of everyone at the table. They turned fearful, questioning eyes on the psychiatrist, grimly aware that a murderer sat among them. DeVries swallowed noisily. "What? Are you mad, lieutenant? You don't know what you're saying—"

"Oh, but I do, Mr. DeVries. The Huntsville police have brought to light your frantic attempts to burn and otherwise destroy the materials that were used in the trial-and-error manufacture of that lethal capsule."

"I didn't agree to a search. Lieutenant, you had no right—"

"A duly processed warrant gave us the right, Mr. DeVries. Besides, you were careless in more ways than one." She drew the blue plastic prescription folder from an inside pocket of her jacket and held it out to him. "If you look carefully at the inside of the third empty celluloid pocket in the row of three, dated May 9th, you will see that the Lab has dusted for a credible thumb print. There just isn't any way a print could get there after the pocket had been sealed, or resealed, as the case may be. What possible reason, Mr. DeVries, can you give for having tampered with a sealed capsule in your mother's prescription folder, other than to rig it for detonation?"

"Oh, Karl—" Elsa DeVries' gaunt face was the color of chalk, her voice a thin filament of fear.

"Shut up, Elsa." DeVries, too, had paled under his scraggly beard. "What you say, lieutenant, is absurd. Why, in heaven's name, would I kill my own mother?"

"I can only answer that question by conjecture, Mr. DeVries." The other members of the family watched and listened in stunned silence. I suggest that you were alienated from your mother the day she married Walter J. Endicott, years ago, when you were still a child. Only the existence of your father's fortune could have persuaded you, over the years to remain close to a mother you felt had sullied the memory of your father. You felt betrayed; her love for you diluted, and divided; first by the man she married, then successively by each child she bore him."

"Rubbish," DeVries was livid. "Utter nonsense."

"It was the proposed reading of your mother's will," the lieutenant went on, "that finally fanned the long-smoldering hatred into a murderous flame. This was your money (or so you envisaged), left to you, in your mother's care. Now it was to be divided among the progeny of your mother's shame. The signing of the will, last night, was to have been a demonstration by Mrs. Endicott, of her impartial love and respect for each of you. But you, Mr. DeVries, did not see it quite that way."

"But how would Karl stand to gain by the death of my mother, lieutenant?" Herman J. was visibly shaken.

"Not at all, monetarily. The ultimate disposition of the estate, which will now go to probate, will not (in my opinion) differ substantially from the provisions already proposed by your mother. But while the money was undoubtedly the catalyst, it was not the motive. Hatred, Mr. Endicott, long-nurturing hatred, can be eminently more obsessive and violent a motive than simple greed."

Elsa DeVries' hawk-like features suddenly slackened into a convoluted mask of fear and remorse. "Karl," she cried, "it's no use—"

The bearded academic glared heatedly at his distracted wife. "Damn you," he seethed. "Damn you all!" His eyes darted wildly about the table from one startled face to another. "Bastards. That's what you are. An illegitimate pack of thieving bastards. You have

no more right to the DeVries fortune than you have to the name—"
After a time, his anger subsided, slowly, into a subdued, breathless sobbing.

"Mrs. DeVries." The lieutenant placed her hand gently on the woman's arm. "It was you, was it not, who procured the capsule blanks for your husband? Did he, perhaps, threaten you?"

"Yes." She hesitantly covered the lieutenant's hand with one of her own, as though seeking a new ally in the face of her husband's anger. "He knew I had access to any number of them, all sizes, from the pharmaceutical firm where I used to work."

The lieutenant's voice, when she spoke, was soothingly quiet. "Do you want to tell us about it?"

The distraught woman glanced apprehensively at her irate husband, wondering whether to proceed. In quick response, the lieutenant caught the eye of Too Tall Bones, "Take this man into another room, officer. Cuff him and detain him, out of earshot."

The scraggly professor sprang to his feet. "You're not getting rid of me that easily," he fumed. "You!" He glared at his wife. "You're no better than the rest of them." He lunged across the table at her, but she cowered away from him like a frightened ostrich.

At that instant, the Amazon's left hand flashed out with the speed of lightning. She caught the one extended wrist closest to her in a grip of steel. She squeezed. And as her knuckles whitened, the pallid face beneath the beard contorted with pain, and the struggling body slumped against the table, limp and helpless.

Moments later, Too Tall Bones was snapping on the cuffs while assessing his amazing colleague with wide, white eyes. "My, my—" he said, with undisguised awe and admiration. And with a puzzled, wondering, final glance at the Amazon, he yanked the disheveled academic to his feet and led him whimpering from the room.

"You were saying, Mrs. DeVries."

As her husband withdrew, the veil of terror that had so quickly cloaked the beady, bird-like eyes, appeared now to lift. "What is it you want to know, lieutenant?"

The lieutenant opened the prescription folder on the table and extracted a capsule. She held it up so that all could see it. "It was a capsule, then, identical to this, that a .22 caliber short round—"

"Two capsules, lieutenant. One, slightly smaller than this, was telescoped into the other, to provide a more solid sheath."

"Then the bullet?"

"Not exactly. A conventional round would have been too long, and too heavy. Karl removed the heavy lead slug and filled the cavity with a weightless cotton fluff, then capped it with a thin disk of a soft lead alloy. But before that, he had weakened the detonating cap by plying it with a kind of acid solution, softening the metal to a point where the slightest impact would set it off."

"Kind of like a hair trigger," the lieutenant suggested. "The spoiled casings of those he had been experimenting with, were found in his workshop. But, tell me, Mrs. DeVries, how was it detonated?"

The other five people at the table leaned forward, straining to catch each tremulously spoken word.

"A small, tightly coiled spring, that had been shaped at one end to facilitate a 'firing pin', was imbedded in the end of the capsule, in line with the detonating cap. It was held there in a specially molded 'saddle' of coated gelatin. This 'coating' effect, lieutenant, is achieved by treating common gelatin with a methanal solution, which causes it to 'harden' and become less soluble when subjected to the gastric juices of the stomach. Variations of this process are widely used today in the manufacture of 'time-release' medications."

"Yes, we're all familiar with them, but—"

"Yes, lieutenant, I'm getting to it. The spring was secured in the coiled position by a 'keeper' of untreated gelatin, leaving it vulnerable to the first eroding effects of the stomach fluids."

"Ah—now I see." The lieutenant held the capsule curiously between thumb and forefinger. "The keeper was designed to dissolve first, while the balance of the capsule was essentially still intact. Then the spring, when released, would propel the firing pin forward, against the detonating cap, and zaaap!"

She tossed the capsule lightly in her hand. "Ingenious, to say the least. The deep red color of the capsule would, of course, hide its contents. It would be a simple matter, then, to substitute the deadly capsule for any other in the prescription folder, and thereby predict the very time of death."

She hesitated a moment, her eyes narrowed in retrospection. The manner of Mrs. Endicott's death, however, the so-called 'exit wound', was simply a matter of chance. Had the device been facing any other way but forward when it exploded, there probably would have been no exterior wound at all. Death, however, would have been just as swift, and just as permanent."

Elsa DeVries reacted with an agonizing moan. "He made me do it, lieutenant. I didn't want to. I—I loved her—"

"Whatever."

The lieutenant nodded to officer Fisk who came forward to escort the sobbing woman from the room. She turned to the others at the table. "That wraps it up," she said curtly. "You are all free to go."

Stunned and shaken by the bizarre turn of events, the five remaining Endicotts filed silently from the room. When only Mark remained, the lieutenant said, "I hope God won't get me for that one little white lie."

"You mean the one about the fingerprint?"

"That's the one. But how did you know?"

"Lieutenant." It was Mark's turn to look pained. "Those capsule pockets are only half an inch in diameter. It would have had to be the thumb of a leprechaun to make contact with one of those concave inner surfaces." He held up his own stubby thumb in evidence.

"Hmm." The lieutenant grinned. "It's plain to see a leprechaun is something you ain't."

"Well," Mark was looking pleased with himself, "you've got to admit I was on the ball—and I didn't give your little game away."

"Ball, you say? Game?" Cathy Carruthers, the earthling, widened her beautiful eyes in mock naivety. "How about that? I thought you were never going to ask."

Hallowe'en Madness

Originally published in *Mike Shane Mystery Magazine*, October 1982.

IT WAS HALLOWE'EN. JACK-O'-LANTERNS GRINNED LIKE orange sharks from darkened windows and elfin monsters roamed freely through the streets. Covens of witches, ghouls and goblins converged on porch-lit doorways with gaping sacks and happy cries of "trick or treat!" It was a time of innocent masquerade. The long dark hours of revelry, mischief and mayhem had not yet begun in Metro. Or so it might have seemed.

Six year-old Tammy O'Toole, alias Wolf Man, her tight blonde curls betraying her presence behind the fright mask, arrived home a few minutes past seven with a sack full of treats. She removed the mask and her heavy outer clothing, then dumped the contents of the sack out over the kitchen table, and began to sort her garnered treasure into piles. When Maureen O'Toole entered the kitchen a few minutes later, she saw her daughter peering intently at a small object about the size and shape of her own lipstick tube.

"Mummy, what's this?"

Maureen took the thing in question between thumb and forefinger and held it up curiously. Her eyes suddenly widened in horror as recognition dawned, and with a violent shudder she let it fall back to the table.

"Oh my God! It's a human finger."

In the Homicide Division of Metro Central's Eleventh Precinct, at precisely 7:29 P.M., Detective-Sergeant Mark Swanson returned the telephone to its cradle and shoved himself away from his desk. He covered the distance to the glass-partitioned office of his immediate superior in three quick strides, rapped twice and entered.

Detective-Lieutenant Cathy Carruthers looked up as Mark's heavily-muscled six-foot frame filled the doorway. She watched him dump himself unceremoniously into a chair and assume a comfortable slouch before she said "Come in," with obvious sarcasm, adding, "is there a law, Mark, that prevents you from closing doors?"

Mark gave the door a jab with one of his size twelves and grimaced as he waited for the slam. When it come, he grinned sheepishly at the lieutenant, then quickly tried to divert her mood, "We've got ourselves a beaut, lieutenant. There's a real weirdo out there tonight."

The lieutenant leveled her vivid blue eyes at him. "Something of a weirdo has just invaded my office," she said with a feisty mix of annoyance and amusement, "Would you care to convince me otherwise?"

Mark produced a cigarette and a wooden match. He ignited the match with a flick of his thumbnail and considered his beautiful partner through a haze of smoke. It had been a good year since he had teamed up with Cathy Carruthers. This remarkable six-foot blonde beauty possessed all the physical attributes of a Playboy Bunny plus a hidden wellspring of such uncanny strength and intelligence that her burly colleagues in Homicide had dubbed her The Amazon, a manifestation of their incredulity, respect and affection. But only to Mark, her trusted and self-appointed side-kick, had she ever permitted a glimpse of the warm and vital woman behind the epithet. And even to him, rarely.

"I just took a call," Mark began, with a heavy pull on his cigarette, "from a Mrs. Maureen O'Toole, out in the old section of East Metro. Says her daughter came home with a sack full of Hallowe'en goodies about twenty minutes ago, and when she dumped it all out on the kitchen table, there was a lady's finger in amongst the candy bars and popcorn balls."

"So? I'm rather fond of lady fingers myself."

"This, lieutenant, was a lady's finger, as in fore, index, ring, or little."

"That's a little gross, isn't it? Are you sure it's not just a hoax, Mark, a plastic or rubber counterfeit?"

"No hoax, lieutenant. No counterfeit."

"Oh, wow! So now we've got a finger freak to go along with the crazies who bury razor blades, broken glass and fishhooks in Hallowe'en handouts. The lieutenant's usually inscrutable features betrayed her extreme abhorrence to these senseless attacks on innocent children. "But, Mark, what are we doing with this call? We're supposed to be handling homicides, remember?"

"Yeah, well, there have been two similar calls within the last half hour, from distraught parents who found 'fingers' in their kids' Hallowe'en haul. Black-and-whites have already checked out both calls, and radioed back in a verification that the fingers were, in fact, genuine—uh, human. So Chief Heller instructed the Desk to route any further calls through to Homicide. He says there's got to be at least one body out there to go with the pinkies, and he wants us to find it."

"Mmmm." The lieutenant got to her feet and began to pace. "That's a little like handing Robbery a couple of hubcaps and asking them to come up with a stolen car."

"At least they'd know the year and make," Mark put in.

"That's true, Mark, but hubcaps don't have fingerprints, at least not their own. Where are those first two fingers now?"

"One was on ice in the Lab when I got the call. The other was on its way in."

"Good. Get down there right away and have a set of prints sent over to Records for a possible match-up. And, Mark, are Fisk and Mayhew on tonight?"

"Yeah—" Mark tugged his eyes up three pulchritudinous levels to a face that was becomingly furrowed in deep thought. "I spotted them in the squad room as I came on tonight."

"Okay. So we'll commandeer them for this one. I want the Metro Central and County Morgues checked out for any fingerless corpses, the hospitals for amputations, the Coroner's office for recent exhumation permits, and the Med staff at Metro U for an accounting of all cadavers in their possession, along with all their spare parts, during the past seventy-two hours."

Mark levered his rugged carcass out of the chair. "Are we going to take that O'Toole call, lieutenant?"

"Indeed, we are. I'll meet you down in the garage in, say, five minutes. That will give you time to reach Fisk and Mayhew, and me to get through to the M.E. Sam Morton's been bragging for years how he came up with the sex, the approximate age, the build and weight, and even the probable occupation of one leg bone—a femur, that had been salvaged from the Metro Dump. I wouldn't like to miss this opportunity to see what he can do with three severed fingers."

"Aren't we jumping the gun, lieutenant, in assuming that all three fingers came from the same hand?"

"You've got a point, Mark. But to think otherwise, would suggest that we're dealing with three fingerless corpses, instead of one. Also, all three have been described as lady's fingers, which, at the moment anyway, seems to point to only one victim." The lieutenant gave Mark a grim look. "And there is still one other possible false assumption that we've been making: That the hand and body belonging to those fingers is, in fact, a corpse. Whoever once owned those fingers, Mark, could well be alive and kicking at this very moment."

The telephone sounded before Mark could respond.

"Carruthers."

He watched her beautiful face darken as she held the instrument against her ear. "Right, sergeant. Yes. We'll pick up both calls on the way out." She broke the connection with her other hand and turned to Mark. "Better get with it. That was a report on another finger. Looks like our crazy's having himself a ball tonight."

It was almost 8:30 when the unmarked Chevy pulled up in front of Maureen O'Toole's split-level bungalow. The trick-or-treat crowd had thinned to a few stragglers.

"Don't forget to lock the car," the lieutenant cautioned as she stepped out onto the sidewalk. "I don't want any Hallowe'en pranksters doing a number on us."

"Don't you think it's a little early for that?" Mark countered as he followed her up the walk.

"It wasn't too early an hour ago for some psycho to start handing out human fingers for Hallowe'en treats."

Mark thumbed the doorbell. "You've got a point there," he said grimly. "By the way, I checked the map in the garage while I was waiting for you, and all four of those calls originated in this same general area."

"That's interesting."

The curtain on the door was drawn aside and a pretty face looked out at them. Mark said "Police," and flashed his badge. The face disappeared and a moment later the door swung open.

"Mrs. O'Toole?"

"Yes. Please come in."

Maureen O'Toole was a typically attractive blue-eyed colleen. She was all of five-feet-two, with abundant auburn hair and a slender engaging figure. She led the two detectives into the kitchen, where six year-old Tammy was still busy with her now slightly depleted hoard of goodies.

"This," Maureen O'Toole said proudly, "is my daughter, Tammy."

The lieutenant took a chair beside the child, which brought her down to eye level and made her seem a little less imposing. "Hello, Tammy. I'm Lieutenant Carruthers, and this is my partner, Sergeant Swanson."

"Hi," she said, ignoring Mark altogether. "Are you a lady detective?"

"Yes, I am."

"He's not."

There was a thread of belligerence in the girl's voice as she shot a quick glance in Mark's direction. Mark looked mildly surprised. He usually got along well with kids.

The lieutenant reached for the child's hand. "We girls have to stick together, don't we, Tammy?"

"Uh-hu."

"'Specially when we're doing detective work, right?"

"Right."

"Well then, do you think you could tell the sergeant, for me, exactly where you went tonight? The names of the streets? The blocks you covered? Like that?"

"I guess so."

Mark took out his notebook and sat down on the other side of the youngster. "Sergeant Swanson at your service, Tammy," he said with a quick salute and a smile. "Ready when you are."

The lieutenant got to her feet then, and Maureen O'Toole headed for the refrigerator. "I scooped it up into a plastic container and put it in the fridge like the sergeant said." She reached in and took out a plastic medicine vial about three inches high by an inch and a half in diameter. "Who could do such an awful thing, lieutenant?"

"We don't have an answer to that yet, Mrs. O'Toole, but we will, in due course."

"It's enough to give a person the creeps," the young woman said nervously.

The lieutenant eyed her closely. "Is your husband not at home tonight, Mrs. O'Toole?"

"My husband and I are separated, lieutenant. The Family Court served him with a restraining order about six weeks ago, to keep him away from Tammy. He had been, uh—" she lowered her eyes, "—abusing her. You know what I mean? Intimately—"

"I understand." But Cathy Carruthers, the woman, did not, in truth, understand at all. She looked wonderingly at the natural warmth and beauty of this young wife and mother, and the sweet innocence of her child, and she questioned how any man could deviate so far from the norm as to willfully forfeit such a treasure. In an effort then, to reify her somber thoughts, she pried the top off the small container and peered in at the severed finger. It was pitifully shrunken, a dirty ashen-gray thing, and it looked grotesquely alone and purposeless lying there in its plastic sheath. It was, nevertheless, unmistakenly a human finger.

Later, as they were leaving, the lieutenant said, "Mrs. O'Toole, where is your husband living now?"

"He has an apartment downtown, close to the Metro General Hospital. That's where he works."

"What are his duties at the hospital?"

"He's an orderly, in O.R."

"O.R.?"

"That's what they call the wing where the operating rooms are located. He actually works in Recovery, which is on the same floor."

"Thank you, Mrs. O'Toole."

When Mark and the lieutenant were back in the car, Mark said, "That little tyke sure covered a wide area. We've got somewhere between three and five square blocks to check out, door-to-door."

"If the kid can do it, Mark, so can Metro P.D. Besides, we should have it narrowed right down by tomorrow morning."

"How so?"

"We received four phone calls, Mark, reporting on four dismembered fingers, that were allegedly picked up by four separate kids, right?"

"Right."

"Well then, if we can assume that each kid covered roughly the same area that Tammy did—"

"—we'll have four times the area to check out," Mark cut in, "about twelve to fifteen blocks in all. It's getting worse all the time."

"Not really, Mark. Those kids might have all started out tonight to trick-or-treat from totally different locations, but you said yourself that all four fingers were given out in the same general area. This would suggest to me, that some of the houses in the overall area would have been visited by more than one of the kids, some houses by more than two, and some, presumably, by more than three. And if we can give any statistical credence to Bernoulli's famous Law of Averages, there would be relatively few in the latter group that were called on by all four kids. And they, Mark, are the only houses that should interest us."

"Lieutenant," Mark groaned, "you're snowing me again. I've got to agree with your reasoning, but how do we go about putting a handle on only those houses that all four kids went to by pure chance?"

"That's the easy part, Mark. And one simple, graphic method of doing it, would be to draw out the route that was taken by each of the kids, to scale, on separate sheets of paper, then superimpose them, one on top of the other, over a street map of the total area. The houses we'd be looking for would be located only at those points where all four of the routes intersected and/or overlapped."

Mark studied his beautiful partner silently for several moments through a one-eyed squint. "Lieutenant, you must have been sired by a mother-lovin' computer." He let out a long sighing breath. "Now tell me, if that was easy, what's the hard part?"

"Getting the information from the kids to make up the four route maps."

"Yeah, I'll buy that one. I just hope they're all as articulate as little Tammy. And, lieutenant, speaking of Tammy, that kid sure seems to have a thing going against anyone who isn't female. I've never had any trouble relating to kids before tonight."

"Nothing to do with you, Mark. She's a victim of that ever-growing malady: child abuse. Her father, in fact, is currently on a restraining order."

"Do tell? And he works at the Metro General in O.R.? Maybe we've got ourselves a fish, lieutenant."

"Maybe. But it's a little early yet to start counting our chickens. Or should I say, fingers?"

Mark grunted dispassionately. "Where do we go from here, lieutenant?"

"I think we'd better pick up that fourth finger before checking out the other calls for route maps."

Mark sighed as he turned the ignition key and slipped the gearshift into Drive. "Something tells me this is going to be a lo-o-ong night."

It was the following day, 11:33 in the A.M., and Mark stood at the entrance to the Metro Central City Morgue watching his favorite police person approach him from the direction of the parking lot. The sinewy grace of Cathy Carruthers as she narrowed the distance between them, her long loping stride, and the superb blend of movement between hip and shoulder was, he mused, a symphony of anatomical perfection. His trance-like abstractions ended abruptly, however, as she bore down on him with a wide smile and a congenial "Hi."

"Hi, yourself."

Mark swung into step beside her as they entered the building and started down a long marble-lined hall. Their voices and footsteps echoed off the high cold walls.

"I asked you to meet me here, Mark, because I thought you'd enjoy being a witness to the big cop-out."

"Cop-out? I don't get it, lieutenant."

"Mark, Sam's been bragging for years about the time he solved the case of the phantom femur, single-handed, by coming up with a make on the murder victim from his examination of a single thigh bone. The way he tells it, he saved the day for the prosecution by making it possible to comply in supersedeas with the court's imposition of a writ of habeas corpus."

"It all sounds Greek to me," Mark said, stifling a yawn.

"Well, it's not. It's Latin. Anyway, first thing this morning, I had the Lab send our four phantom fingers over to Sam's office with a requisition for an 'identity prognosis'. I thought I'd give him an opportunity, once and for all, to put up or shut up."

"You don't think he can do it?"

"Let's just say that I think his tales are taller than his track record."

At the door labeled: SAMUEL MORTON, M.D., CORONER AND CHIEF MEDICAL EXAMINER, M.C.P.D., they knocked and entered. Sam Morton, short, balding and grumpy, looked up over thick-rimmed spectacles from behind his desk.

"Ah, Metro's finest. I've been expecting you."

The lieutenant caught Mark's eye with a confiding wink. "What have you got for us, Sam?"

The M.E. shoved his glasses up higher up on the bridge of his nose and reached across his desk for a brown manilla file folder. "Now understand," he said preemptively, "we can't expect too much from the examination of a mere finger—"

"Uh—just a moment, Sam." The lieutenant, Mark knew, was going to milk this little scenario for all it was worth. "I think Mark had better get all this down. We know your reputation in the field, and I wouldn't care to trust to memory—"

"Forget it!" Sam scowled. "You can take the bloody file with you when you go. Now—you want to hear this, or not?"

"Whenever you're ready, Sam."

"—but," the M.E. glanced up, ready to thwart a further interruption, and when it didn't come, he continued, "in view of the fact that, on this occasion, I had (not one, but) four fingers to work with, and I was able to establish almost at once that all four were from the same hand, my prognostications were accordingly somewhat routine and (I add in all modesty), substantive."

The lieutenant gave Mark a look that seemed to begin somewhere in Texas and end up in Missouri.

"I'm going to skip the gobbledygook on techniques and methods (you probably wouldn't understand them anyway) and get right down to a biological reconstruction of the disjecta membra in question."

"The what?" Mark muttered.

"More Latin," the lieutenant told him with a grin.

Sam Morton ignored the interruption. "My tests have shown this alleged victim to be a fair-haired, light-complexioned, female Caucasian, approximately eight years of age, rather slight in build and of average height for her years. She either resided, or attended school, in the greater Metro area, and was, at the time of her dismemberment, connected in some meaningful way with the modeling of clay."

He looked up from his notes to see the lieutenant's open mouth snap shut, then wreathe into a smile of genuine approval and esteem.

"That's incredible, Sam. I owe you an apology. I do. I really didn't think—"

Sam Morton closed the file with an ill-humored growl. "What did you expect, for Chrissake—chopped liver?"

"I don't know what I expected," the lieutenant laughed uncertainly, "but it wasn't this. I'd take my hat off to you, Sam, if I had one on. I don't suppose you'd care to enlighten us on how you arrived at those conclusions?"

The crusty M.E. sighed indulgently. "It's all here in the file," he grumbled, "but, okay. In layman's terms: the hair color, complexion and the Caucasian factor is determined by skin pigmentation; the sex, age, height and general build, by bone analysis and growth projection; her domicile and probable hobby, from under-nail residues; and the approximate time of dismemberment, by cellular decomposition."

"Time of dismemberment?"

"Oh—I didn't mention that, did I? Those fingers were severed from the hand to which they were once attached, lieutenant, about a year ago."

"A year ago?" The lieutenant could not contain her surprise. "Then how have they been so well preserved?"

"They've been frozen." The M.E. smiled patiently. And that was deduced from cellular fragmentation in both the epidermis and the muscle fiber itself—"

"Enough already—" The lieutenant was suddenly all business. She reached across the desk for the file folder. "You say it's all in here?"

"It's all there, and it's all yours."

At he door, the lieutenant paused and turned. "Sam." She appeared to be a little discomfited. "I'd just like you to know that it's good to have you on the team."

When the door had closed behind them, SAMUEL MORTON, M.D., Coroner and Chief Medical Examiner, M.C.P.D., shrugged off a fleeting smile and went on with his work.

12:57 P.M. The top of Mark's desk was hidden under an enlarged street map of East Metro. On one portion of the map, three squares of transparent drafting paper had been thumb-tacked into position, one above the other. At an adjacent desk, the department artist was drawing out to scale, the fourth and final route on a similar square of tissue. Mark stood over the man, watching the red line that was Tammy O'Toole's route last night, lengthen in an irregular loop that zig-zagged over the paper, then doubled back on itself to the point where it started.

"There. That does it, Mark. Let's get this last one pegged out on the big map."

The route of each Hallowe'en trick-or-treater had been drawn in with a different color. Blue, green, yellow, and now red. The lines spidered through the streets of East Metro, intersecting and overlapping at numerous points, but only on three short block-long streets, in an "H"-shaped configuration, did all four colors come together.

"That nails it down to just three short blocks," Mark grunted appreciably. "See what you can do, O'Malley, when you've got a God-given brain instead of a shillelagh between your ears?"

O'Malley lifted one disparaging eyebrow in Mark's direction, gathered up his paraphernalia, and walked away without comment. Lieutenant Carruthers paused and turned as she came into the room, just in time to watch the artist stomp angrily out the door.

"What's with O'Malley?" she said to Mark.

"Search me, lieutenant. Maybe somebody crumpled his crayons."

The lieutenant grinned. "Guess who," she said. She tossed Mark one of two paper sacks she carried. "I bought you some lunch. A couple of salamis and a danish. I thought we'd eat in and save time."

"You're all heart," Mark muttered.

"Any success on the search pattern?"

"Yeah—we've got it narrowed down to three single blocks."

"Good. We'll get Fisk and Mayhew on it." She glanced at her watch. "They were due in here at one."

As though on cue, officer Mayhew and policewoman Fisk appeared at the door. The lieutenant beckoned them with a tilt of her chin. "You better get in on this," she said to Mark.

"First off," the lieutenant began when they were all seated, "I'd like to hear what you came up with last night."

"One big zero," Mayhew said.

"With the ring removed," Fisk added for emphasis.

"You covered all the ground?"

"We started with the city morgue," Mayhew explicated, "then those in the County as far as Ridgewood. We had to take on two extra men—"

"Persons," Fisk put in.

"—to cover the hospitals (the Chief okayed it, lieutenant), and the Coroner's office informed us that there had been no disinterments in the last three months. Finally, Fisk and I finished it off this morning with a trip out to Metro U. It was zilch all the way, lieutenant."

"Well, that's not surprising, I guess," Mark said with perverse good humor, "when you consider that the mutilations we're looking for, happened a year ago."

"What?" Mayhew did a double-take on Mark, then addressed the lieutenant. "Then what were we doing—?"

"Relax," Mark grinned, "we just got the news, late this morning."

Fisk looked disheartened, "So now we've got to do it all over again, in a wider time frame—" She made a sour face and shuddered. "—ugh, I guess it's back to those horrible cadavers."

"That might not be necessary." The lieutenant chuckled at the young brunette in spite of herself. "We've got a door-to-door for you today—"

Mayhew groaned.

"—and where you go from there will depend on what you come up with."

Fisk brightened. "Anything," she said emphatically, "would be an improvement on going shopping for fingers in that human-parts department at Metro U."

The lieutenant drew back a fall of golden hair that had strayed over her forehead. "Line them up on that map, Mark, so they can get on it right away." To Fisk and Mayhew, she said, "Take your hand-radios with you and keep in close contact. Report anything, anything, that appears in any way irregular."

"You got it, lieutenant."

When Mark returned a few minutes later, the lieutenant had her elbows spread before her on the desk with her fingers interlocked and her chin resting on the backs of her hands. "I've got a hunch," she said.

"Uh-hu." A hunch with Cathy Carruthers, Mark knew, was not a hunch at all, but a well-considered expectation. When he had settled back comfortably in his customary slouch, he said, "Are you going to tell me about it?"

The lieutenant looked at him, moving only her eyes. "I think it's a Hallowe'en thing," she said.

"How about that?" Mark thumped his forehead with the heel of his hand. "I wonder where I got side-tracked into thinking that this was the Fourth of July?"

The lieutenant appeared (or chose) not to hear him. "I believe this is more than just the twisted humor of a Hallowe'en sickie, Mark. I think this is the second chapter in a two-part drama, one that began, perhaps, a year ago, or longer—but whenever it was, and whatever it was, it's got Hallowe'en written all over it."

Mark began to munch on a salami sandwich. "What makes you think there's more here than meets the eye, lieutenant?"

"I should have brought something to drink with this," the lieutenant said absently as she unwrapped one of her sandwiches.

"How about some battery-acid from the local urn?" Mark offered.

"I guess we don't have much choice."

Mark had returned with the coffee and settled down once again into his awkward slouch, before the lieutenant responded to his initial question.

"To begin with, Mark, there isn't anything very casual or spontaneous about freezing four severed fingers for an entire year before handing them out on Hallowe'en as trick-or-treats."

"Maybe they were already frozen," Mark suggested, "and whoever it was, just thought about the trick-or-treat bit at the last minute."

"Yes. but why freeze them in the first place?"

"I see what you mean."

"And then, there's the ghoulish fact that these fingers are not even from an adult hand, but from the hand of an eight year-old girl. A mere child."

"Yeah. You'd think if a kid that age had lost all her fingers, alive or dead, we'd have heard about it."

"That's just it, Mark. Maybe we have heard about it. Maybe we just haven't made the connection."

"Lieutenant." Mark spoke around a mouthful of salami. "Don't you think you're reaching just a little? You're saying that something might have happened, but you don't know what, last year at Hallowe'en, maybe, connected in some way with the severed fingers, perhaps—Jeeeeez! We don't even know who the victim is, much less the killer. That is, if there is a killer."

"The trouble with you, Mark, is you don't have a woman's intuition."

"I wonder why?" Mark muttered as he started in on his danish.

The lieutenant reached for the telephone and dialed an inside line. "Garfield? This is—oh, you recognize my voice—"

Mark polished off the rest of his danish and his coffee as he listened to his senior partner clue in Garfield Leprohn (the Leprechaun, as he was known to his department cohorts) on the known details of the case. The Leprechaun had the dubious distinction of being the shortest policeman on the Metro Force, "or any other force," Mark had once suggested, "with the possible exception of Gravity." He went four-foot zilch in his sweat sox and, happily for the Leprechaun, he had been hired to head the Records Department on the strength of his data-gathering status, rather than his stature. Mark took a perverse pleasure in needling the little man at every opportunity.

"I suggested to him," the lieutenant said when she had hung up the phone, "that he start down in the 'morgue' at the Metro Examiner. If he draws a blank there, he's always got his own Data-Bank in Records to fall back on."

"Still playing your hunch?"

"What else have I got to play with?"

Mark looked wonderingly at his beautiful colleague and opened his mouth to respond, but didn't. There were times, he decided with some reluctance, that discretion really was the better part of valor, not to mention its amorous equivalent.

It was nineteen minutes past five o'clock when the Leprechaun put out a call for Lieutenant Carruthers. She and Mark were in the unmarked Chevy, heading back to H.Q. after a field check on Fisk and Mayhew. The voice of the girl in Dispatch crackled through the car radio.

"Message for Lieutenant Carruthers. Respond, please." The staccato buzz of the radio took over briefly.

"Carruthers here. Proceed."

"Lieutenant. The Lepre—uh, Corporal Leprohn has important information for you and requests your location."

"No need. We're on our way in. Instruct the Corporal to wait."

"Yes, Mam. Can you give me an E.T.A.?"

"Five minutes."

"Yes, Mam. Over and out."

When the lieutenant hung up the mike, Mark said, "It sounds like our Irish elf might have come up with something."

The lieutenant nodded speculatively. "I'm counting on it," she said.

The Leprechaun was at his desk in the Records Department when the lieutenant and Mark burst in on him. The little cop grinned up at them, delighted to once again be the center of attention. "Have a seat," he said, "I've got a story to tell."

"Just keep it pertinent and concise," the lieutenant said a little impatiently.

"He only tells short stories," Mark reassured her. "As a matter of fact—"

"Mark." The one word, quietly spoken, was enough to still her partner's wily wit as he hunkered down into his usual happy slouch with a wide-eyed look of innocence. The lieutenant then turned her own startling blue eyes on the Leprechaun. "Let's have it," she said.

"Well, you were right, lieutenant, about it being a Hallowe'en caper." The Leprechaun handed the lieutenant a number of photo-copy sheets from an open file on his desk. "These are copies of a story that broke in the morning edition of the Huntsville Herald, exactly one year ago today. I started with the Examiner, as you suggested, but drew a blank. I tried the Huntsville paper on a hunch, even though it is over the state line. There were follow-ups on the story, both in the Herald and on television, but I don't think we picked up much of it in Metro. But I am certain, lieutenant, that this story has some connection with the severed fingers that were handed out last night here in Metro as Hallowe'en treats."

"There's a lot of reading here, Garfield." The lieutenant flipped through the photo-copies. "Suppose you give us a brief summary."

The Leprechaun settled back with a see-who's-got-the-floor-now look at Mark, and after an annoying preemtive cough and a meaningfully bated pause, he began his story.

"On Hallowe'en," he said, "last year, eight year-old Cindy Crawford started out in Huntsville on her trick-or-treat rounds. It was about 6:30 P.M. and already dark. Cindy was dressed as "Mary" of Mary-Had-A-Little-Lamb fame, and her pint-sized poodle, Piddles, was dolled up as the lamb. Piddles was a Heinz-57 variety purebred and Cindy had him on a leash. In the course of her rounds, Cindy was apparently lured, on some pretext that was never made totally clear, into a seldom-used lane by a couple of eager pubescent boys dressed as Pirates. One of the boys had a real sword as part of his costume, a souvenir his father had brought back from Nam, and when young Cindy resisted their less-than-honorable intentions (can you believe it, lieutenant, at that age?), the boys threatened to decapitate her 'little lamb' unless she became more cooperative."

The Leprechaun paused for a breath and for oratorical effect, which managed to evoke a stifled yawn from Mark and a weary sigh from the lieutenant.

"It was all a tasteless prank, of course, but it turned suddenly sour. The boys had no intention of actually harming the dog, but as the sword descended, and Cindy reached out unexpectedly to save her precious Piddles—well, the rest is history. The dog was released at the last moment and the sword struck the girl's outstretched hand, lopping it off at the wrist. Cindy passed out and the boys fled in disbelief and horror. The bottom line was: by the time Cindy was found, about two hours later, by a neighbor and his wife out walking their mutt, she had bled to death. The boys were ferreted out the next day and confessed readily. Because of their ages, however, they were given suspended sentences, which apparently sent Crawford, Cindy's father, into a public tirade. Cindy's mother had been killed in a traffic accident about eighteen months prior to the Hallowe'en tragedy and the little girl was all he had left in the world. It was a rough scene for the poor guy."

The lieutenant looked sadly into space and spoke slowly, softly, as though from memory,

"But when to mischief mortals bend their will,

How soon they find fit instruments of ill.

Alexander Pope said that at the turn of the eighteenth century, Mark," she said. "Things haven't really changed all that much, have they?"

The Leprechaun was fidgeting impatiently. "There's more to it, lieutenant. While we weren't able to establish an I.D. from the fingerprints sent to us by the Lab, we did learn that both Cindy and her father were engaged in a pottery making project just prior to her death."

"That could be all the identification we need, at this point, anyway."

"Maybe so, but here's the clincher. The neighbor who found the girl, sent his wife home to phone the police, then remained at the scene to wait for them. He was there when the police arrived."

"So?"

"So to this day, lieutenant, they have never found that severed hand."

"Hmmm. And you're suggesting that maybe the neighbor took it?"

"I'm not suggesting anything, lieutenant. I'm merely pointing out that the only person who was alone with that girl, after the hand had been severed, was, in fact, the neighbor."

"Who in hell would want to steal a hand?" Mark said in disgust. "And why?"

"Why, indeed," the lieutenant said thoughtfully. "do you have an address on Crawford, Garfield?"

"Yes. And the neighbor, too." The Leprechaun scrawled both addresses on a sheet of canary-yellow and handed it across the desk. "And here's where it all starts to come together. Crawford, you'll notice, moved to Metro about six months ago and now lives on the south-west leg of that search pattern you've got mapped out on Mark's desk. The Crawford house is at the end of the street—"

The lieutenant got quickly to her feet. "I wish you had mentioned this earlier," she said with obvious concern, "Fisk and Mayhew should be half way down that street about now, and they could be heading into trouble. Get a back-up out there for them right away, Mark, and let them know we're on our way."

"You got it, lieutenant, but what makes you think there's any urgency about this? I mean, we still don't even know what happened to that hand—"

"Oh, come now, Mark. I think it's fairly obvious what must have happened to the hand. I'm surprised they didn't pick it up a year ago. Now get that back-up team out to the Crawford address, S.A.P., and tell them to keep out of sight and wait until we get there."

The Leprechaun looked both puzzled and frustrated. "You mean you think Crawford took the hand?"

"No, Crawford didn't take it. There was no way he could have. Nevertheless, I'm fully convinced that it did come into his pos-session. And it's my guess, gentlemen, that he's still got it." The lieutenant sighed grimly. "Or what's left of it."

A full moon had turned the night into an eerie blend of silvered images and black velvet shadows. Mark flicked off the headlights before the unmarked Chevy made a slow turn at the corner, then ghosted to a stop at the curb where a vacant lot made a toothless gap in the row of houses. A black-and-white was parked a few yards ahead of them and Mark watched a towering shadow detach itself from the gloom and approach the Chevy.

"That can only be Too-Tall Bones," Mark observed, "either that or Fisk has managed to talk Mayhew into carrying her on his shoulders."

The lieutenant chuckled. As the black giant neared the car, she said, "It's Bones, all right. Run your window down, Mark."

Too-Tall Bones lowered his great head to the level of the open window. When he smiled, his teeth and eyes glowed florescently in the dark.

"Where's Fisk and Mayhew?" the lieutenant asked.

"They're in the next house, lieutenant. The one between the vacant lot and the one on the end. They haven't come out yet."

"How long have they been in there?"

"Better part of twenty minutes," Bones replied, "they were just going in when we got here. Want us to bring 'em out?"

"No." Mark could see the lieutenant shake her golden head by the light of the dash. "We'll wait."

"No need," Mark interjected, "there they are now. I think they've spotted us."

As the two officers approached the car, the lieutenant said to the tall black, "Who are you on with tonight, Bones?"

"Dave Madson, lieutenant. He's right here." Bones moved sufficiently to allow Madson's normal-sized head to appear behind his own. "And Mark," Bones added in a tired voice, "we've already been through the David-and-Goliath routine, so forget it."

The dashboard light did not do justice to Mark's thespian attempt at injured innocence. "Why do I suddenly feel like part of an unsung minority?" he muttered.

When Fisk and Mayhew had joined the group at the car, the lieutenant filled them in on the tragic story of Cindy Crawford.

"Wouldn't you know it," Fisk moaned. "That's the second time in as many days that we've been preempted by a break in the case, after putting in all the leg work."

"Would you rather have spent the day holding hands with the cadavers at Metro U?" Mayhew asked lightly.

"Scheee!" Fisk responded. "What kind of choice is that? Mayhew or the cadavers—?"

The lieutenant climbed out of the car. "Can it, you two." To all five of them, as they gathered around her, she said, "This man Crawford is a psychopath and he may be dangerous, as much to himself as to any of us. I want him apprehended, unharmed. Remember, he's not so much a criminal as a victim."

"Don't worry, lieutenant," Too-Tall Bones rumbled, "we'll be gentle." Everyone, including the lieutenant, chuckled softly at the St. Bernard-like pathos of the big black.

"Lieutenant," Madson suddenly piped up, "how come there's six of us just to take one lousy looney?"

"That looney, as you call him, Madson, will be pretty well stretched out after hacking off his daughter's fingers to commemorate her untimely death at the hands of a couple of juvenile pirates. He's been licking his emotional wounds for twelve long months, and it's my guess he's just about ready to snap. I don't want anybody taking this guy too lightly. That clear?"

There was a low murmur of assent.

"Okay. Bones, you and Madson take the back of the house. Fisk and Mayhew, one of you on either side. I don't want him slipping out a window on us—"

"What if we're spotted?" Bones wondered.

"Don't be," the lieutenant cautioned tersely.

"No one's going to make you at night, Bones," Mark added, "just so long as you remember not to smile."

The big black's laugh was like a peel of quiet thunder. "There just ain't nothin' sicker'n hunky humor," he muttered as he faded into the surrounding shadows.

The lieutenant and Mark walked slowly down to the front gate of the Crawford house, then stood waiting in the shadows until the others had taken up their positions.

"Wait here, Mark," the lieutenant whispered finally, "and stay out of sight. He'll be less likely to panic if he thinks I'm alone. Just keep me covered."

"You can count on it," Mark assured her.

The moon caught the lieutenant's fleeting smile. "I know I can," she said with feeling. A moment later, she was moving quickly toward the darkened front door of the house.

Mark watched the Lieutenant's dark shape climb the two short steps to the porch and rap heavily on the door. A porch light flicked on after a few tense seconds and a small dog began to yap-yap from somewhere within the house. When the door swung open, Mark could see a heavy, balding man in his middle years, standing behind the now sharply-defined silhouette of the Amazon. He heard her voice faintly, indistinctly, as she spoke to him. He saw her flash her badge.

Then all hell broke loose.

The man in the doorway appeared to turn, slowly, as though to move back into the house, but then, in the next instant, his body exploded into unexpected, violent motion. Mark saw the lieutenant's tall shadow suddenly double forward as the man's knotted fist plowed into her stomach. She let out a grunt of disbelief and pain. Then, before she could straighten, the same fist jerked back and pistoned forward again, this time smashing squarely into her unprotected face.

Mark was already on the move as the Amazon sagged back toward the edge of the porch, but as she fell, she reached out and caught the wrist behind that knotted fist in a vice-like grip. Mark was still thirty feet away when the Amazon hit the lawn. She landed heavily on her shoulders, the man hurtling toward her as he was drawn along by the impetus of her falling weight and her tenacious hold on his wrist. In the space of a split second, Mark saw the Amazon's long silken legs fold in under the plummeting body of the man, then snap violently upward with the force and fluidity of twin hydraulic rams.

Mark jerked to a stop as Crawford went rocketing into space, and he regretted later, that he had been too preoccupied at the time, to fully appreciate that superb launching pad. He was left with only the briefest recollection of those long, sinewy, shimmering thighs and the don't-blink-or-you'll-miss-it flash of white panties, in the talismanic light of a friendly moon.

The blurred and violent impact of Crawford hurtling squarely into his arms, cut off any further voyeuristic delights for Mark. When he had recovered sufficiently from the impact, the lieutenant was snapping the cuffs on a dazed and unresisting Crawford.

Officer Fisk stood in the doorway of Lieutenant Carruthers' office, her soft brown eyes moist with concern. Mayhew's handsome face looked in over her shoulder.

"I'm really sorry about that belt in the eye you took, lieutenant," the young brunette rookie said feelingly.

"Thanks for the sympathy," the lieutenant replied, then added candidly, "but it was the eye in my belt buckle, along with that first punch that did the most damage."

The lieutenant looked for all the world like a movie star holding a press conference, Mark thought as he watched her closely from his usual slouching roost, her beautiful face even more inscrutable behind a pair of dark glasses.

"I've got a St. John's Ambulance ticket, lieutenant," Mayhew said glibly, "if I could be of any—"

A dark threatening glance from Mark and a sharp dig in the ribs from Fisk, cut short Mayhew's less-than-honorable mission of mercy. He flushed uneasily and drifted back out of sight.

"If you're feeling up to it, lieutenant," Fisk interjected quickly, "there's one thing about that Crawford case that still puzzles me."

"And that is?"

"Well, we all know that the guy confessed to having the girl's missing hand, and to ugh cutting off the fingers to hand out as Hallowe'en treats, but I still don't know how he came into possession of the hand in the first place."

"I'm surprised you haven't figured that one out," the lieutenant told her. "It was delivered to him the next morning by Cindy's constant and faithful companion, Piddles."

"The dog?"

"Or, Mary's Little Lamb, if you prefer."

"But why would a dog—?"

"The dog, I'm sure, did not fully appreciate the horror of the situation, although I have little doubt that it knew something was terribly wrong. Cindy, after all, had obviously been hurt. I strongly suspect that Piddles picked up the hand and took it home in an instinctive attempt to summon help. Where the dog hid it then, until Crawford took it from him the following morning, is anybody's guess."

"But then why, in Heaven's name, would he keep the horrible thing for a whole year, then hack it up and hand it out to the trick-or-treaters on Hallowe'en?"

The lieutenant winced as she settled back in her chair. She pressed an immaculately manicured hand gingerly to her stomach. "The hand, remember, was all he had left of his little girl. It was not a 'horrible thing' to him. Still, he wasn't quite sure what to do with it, so he froze it in his home freezer to keep it from spoiling until he was able to make a decision. And that, of course, is where we found what was left of it, last night. I imagine he had thoughts, at first, of digging a private little grave, a memorial, of sorts, to the memory of one who had so suddenly, so tragically been taken from him. This, you'll recall, was his second great loss in the space of eighteen months. Little wonder he finally flipped."

"Then why the mutilations, lieutenant? That just does not seem consistent with the picture you've been painting of unbearable grief."

The lieutenant sighed. "It was the hand, you see, that kept the memory of that night alive and vivid in his mind. His grief had not been given the chance to subside in the natural healing processes of time. When Hallowe'en came around for the second time, it was just too much for him. He had been nurturing and wallowing in this horror for a year, and he wanted some kind of revenge. He wanted to jar the minds and souls of those 'juvenile killers' (his words) with the magnitude of the thing they had done. That he was now living in a different area was of no consequence. The trick-or-treaters everywhere were, in his eyes, all of a kind."

"Fisk." It was Mayhew's voice, calling from the outer room. "You coming, or not?"

"I think Helpful-Harry is getting impatient," the lieutenant said with some amusement.

Officer Fisk flushed prettily. "He's not really like that, lieutenant," she said defensively. "He's—well, he's a helluva partner."

"I'm very much aware of his abilities, Fisk, and yours as well. That's possibly why you find yourselves so frequently on our team."

Fisk beamed. "Well," she stammered, looking pleasantly embarrassed, "duty calls." She left quickly.

Now that they were alone, the lieutenant eased the dark glasses off to reveal a deep purple mouse where her beautiful right eye should have been. "I'm surprised you haven't made some smart-ass remark about this shiner, Mark, or the belt-buckle bruise on my— my abdomen."

"Well, I've seen the shiner, lieutenant, and frankly, it just don't look very funny—"

The lieutenant's one good eye reflected her mute gratitude at his concern.

"—but I haven't yet seen the belt-buckle bruise."

"And you're not likely to. But I can assure you, it isn't very funny either."

"You weren't so wrapped up in false modesty last night," Mark reminded her with a secret smile.

The lieutenant chuckled. "For a moment there, I wasn't wrapped up in much of anything, was I?" She added thoughtfully, "Maybe I should start wearing pant suits."

"Oh, come now," Mark said quickly. "Let's not over-react. I'm sure I can adjust to an occasional lapse of modesty—if I put my mind to it."

Cathy Carruthers had replaced her dark glasses and he could not see her eyes when she replied.

"I'm sure you can."

Enter the lively and lurid world of DIME CRIME!

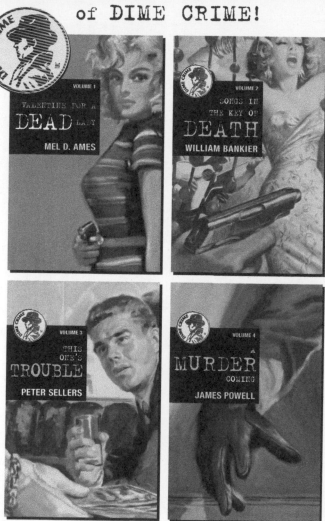

Dime Crime is an exciting new series collecting some of the best crime short stories by many of the legendary and overlooked authors in the genre. To learn more about past and future volumes in the series, or details about the authors and their stories, visit the Dime Crime website for details:

www.dimecrime.com